IF PHYLLIS WERE HERE

GAIL JARROW lives in Ithaca, New York, with her husband, three children, and a rabbit named Leo the Lop. For several years she was a math and science teacher, but now her work time is devoted to writing.

IF PHYLLIS WERE HERE

GAIL JARROW

AN AVON CAMELOT BOOK

AVON BOOKS
A division of
The Hearst Corporation
105 Madison Avenue
New York, New York 10016

Copyright © 1987 by Gail Jarrow
Published by arrangement with Houghton Mifflin Company
Library of Congress Catalog Card Number: 87-3040
ISBN: 0-380-70634-2
RL: 5.3

First Avon Camelot Printing: May 1989

CAMELOT TRADEMARK REG. U.S. PAT. OFF. AND IN OTHER COUNTRIES,
MARCA REGISTRADA, HECHO EN U.S.A.

Printed in the U.S.A.

OPM   10   9   8   7   6   5   4   3   2   1

For Heather
and
her Gram and Mimi

Contents

1   We're Rich!   1

2   The Countdown   11

3   Beetle #50   20

4   Nobody Home   33

5   Mealworm Rendezvous   50

6   One More Annoying Detail   61

7   Going into Business   69

8   Sore Throat   79

9   Trouble Brewing   87

10   A Silver Lining   96

11   Birthday Surprise   104

12   The Frame-Up   110

13   Caught Purple-Handed   119

14   Off with the Hat   127

IF PHYLLIS
WERE HERE

One

We're Rich!

• Phyllis just won the Massachusetts State Lottery. And I'm never again wearing my long-sleeved shirt with the four-leaf clovers.

I had on that shirt the day Phyllis and Mr. Snellenberger took me for a sundae at the Belmont Drugstore and Fountain. The chocolate chip ice cream there is the best in the state — at least in any of the places I've been. Plus, they squirt on a heap of whipped cream. Mr. S. says it reminds him of the Matterhorn in January.

"Let's buy a lottery ticket," Mr. S. said to Phyllis while they stood at the cash register.

She pinched his cheek. "Now, Henry, you know I don't gamble."

"Come on, Pigeon." He squeezed her around the waist.

I took a couple of giant steps toward the magazine

rack and hid my face behind the latest Fantastic Four comic. It was embarrassing to be with them when they acted like that. You'd think they were teenagers instead of septuagenarians. In case you don't know, that means they're seventy years old. Phyllis likes the word because she thinks it sounds dignified.

Phyllis has weird ideas about words. She doesn't let me call her Grandma or Nana because that makes her feel old, which is pretty silly because a septuagenarian *is* old, no matter how you say it.

"Wish us luck." Mr. S. held up the lottery ticket. "We went halfsies. Your grandmother wouldn't let me buy it for her."

"Good luck," I said.

Maybe saying those two words did it. Or maybe it was the dumb shirt with the four-leaf clovers. All I know is Phyllis never won anything in her life before this.

"Quick, Libby, let's turn on the news." Phyllis dried her hands on her apron. "We'll finish cleaning up the kitchen later," she told me. "Can't miss my sixty seconds of fame."

Ever since their ticket won, Phyllis hasn't been herself. Tonight she had made a tuna casserole.

Phyllis *never* makes casseroles. She says it's lazy cooking. I guess she thinks it's okay for millionaires to be lazy.

"I wish Mother hadn't gone to that Bar Association banquet," I said, as we left the kitchen.

"It's a shame that it was scheduled for tonight," agreed Phyllis. "But the others in the law firm were counting on Anne to go. You knew that."

"Yeah, I guess so," I muttered.

"We'll just have to tell her all about it," she said.

My dad sat in the maroon recliner, his favorite chair, feverishly scribbling on a pad of paper. I glanced over his shoulder at the symbols and Greek letters covering the page.

"Phyllis's interview is almost on, Dad."

Silence. More scribbling.

"You wanted to see it."

"Hmmm."

Phyllis picked up the channel selector and flipped on the TV. She looked at Dad. "Must be another hot equation."

When my father is concentrating on his work, which seems to be most of the time he isn't eating or sleeping (sometimes then, too), he tunes out everything around him.

I pulled the beanbag chair toward the TV and plopped down at ringside. "What was it like to be interviewed, Phyllis?"

"A new experience, that's all I can say for it. The reporter asked the most unimaginative questions. You'll see what I mean."

"Got it!" Dad jumped up and waved his paper. "It drove me crazy all day, but I finally realized the assumption was wrong."

"Just in time, Rod," said Phyllis. "My interview's about to start."

"What interview?"

"You know, Phyllis's lottery interview," I explained.

"Oh, right," he said vaguely. He'd completely forgotten that we'd told him about it at dinner. Maybe he never even heard us.

"Here it is." Phyllis turned up the volume.

There she was — my grandmother — on TV, in living color. "Phyllis, I can't believe it!" I squealed.

"Quiet down, Libby, or we'll miss the interview," said Dad.

I stared at the television screen, trying to remember every detail so I could tell my mother. The news team had filmed the interview in front of the Belmont Drugstore, where Phyllis and Mr. S. had bought their winning ticket. The two of them stood next to a blonde woman with a toothy smile and not-a-hair-out-of-place hairdo.

The woman stuck the microphone in front of Phyllis's face. "How does it feel to win a million dollars?" she asked.

"Nothing special," replied Phyllis. Mr. S. grinned and gazed into the camera.

"Hasn't sunk in yet, I bet," the reporter said with a perky voice.

Phyllis shook her head. "No. We haven't seen the money yet. Ask me after the first check arrives."

Mr. S.'s grin expanded. I wondered how far his cheeks could stretch. "What's wrong with Mr. S.?" I asked. "He looks like the Cheshire Cat."

"He was a bit nervous," said Phyllis. "But watch this next part."

"And what do you two plan to do with your winnings?" the TV reporter continued.

Suddenly, Mr. S.'s grin disappeared. He put his arm around Phyllis and kissed her cheek. Why did he have to do *that* on television? "It's none of your business," he snapped.

"Good for him!" Dad laughed.

"She's a real gem, don't you think?" Phyllis said, as

she turned off the set. "Too bad we don't have a VCR. I'd love to have a tape for Anne to see."

"We're rich now, Phyllis. We can buy a VCR. And a new car and a . . ."

"Hold on, Libby," Dad interrupted. "To be precise, it is Phyllis and Mr. S., not *we*, who are rich."

Dad is a nut about precision. He can't help it. He's a mathematician.

"What *are* you going to do with your money?" I asked.

"You're as bad as that dizzy reporter." Phyllis tugged at my arm. "Help me finish loading the dishwasher."

"I'd say Libby has the instincts of a third-rate journalist, Phyllis," said Dad, as he opened the newspaper to the crossword puzzle.

"Good. We won't have to worry about her future anymore." She winked at him.

Very funny. But I still wondered what Phyllis planned to do with all her loot.

My mother finally got home at 10:30. I know because she came in through the back door and woke Samantha and George. Even though their cage is on the side porch, I can hear their squeals way up in my room. For two guinea pigs, they make a lot of racket. When they really let loose, the whole neighborhood hears them.

I figured something was going on as soon as I heard Phyllis's voice in the kitchen below my room. She never stays up past ten, no matter what. Climbing out of bed, I put my ear against the floor.

Their voices were garbled. The only thing I could make out was Dad saying, "What do you think Libby will . . ."

Maybe Phyllis wanted permission to buy me an expensive gift like a ten-speed or a computer or a lifetime subscription to all the Marvel comics.

I watched the red numbers on my digital clock change until the voices stopped and I heard footsteps on the stair. Jumping into bed, I pulled up the covers and closed my eyes. The door opened, and the fragrance of Heaven Scent drifted toward me. I know the perfume's name because I gave it to my mother last Christmas. She kissed my forehead, then quietly closed the door.

The next morning at breakfast the three of them dropped the bomb. They didn't even give me a chance to finish my cereal.

Phyllis and my mother sat on the bench across the

table from me. When you see them side by side, they look almost like twins rather than mother and daughter, although Phyllis is thirty-five years more wrinkled. Same blue eyes, light hair, and petite bodies.

Unfortunately, I missed out on all that. My eyes are green, hair brown, and I'm definitely not petite. I resemble my dad, except I'm not going bald.

"Phyllis has something to tell you, Libby," said my mother. Her hands were folded on the table. The knuckles were white.

"To be precise, we all have something to tell you." Dad flipped a pancake into the air and caught it on the spatula.

"Libby, dear" — Phyllis reached for my hand — "I've decided to move to Florida."

"Florida!" I almost gagged on my Fruit Loops. Milk leaked out the corners of my mouth. I didn't bother wiping it. So much for the expensive gift.

"Yes, the beautiful sunshine state where we get oranges and grapefruits." Phyllis was smiling.

"All by yourself?" I said, hoping she'd laugh and say, "Had you fooled, didn't I? I was only kidding."

"Mr. S. is coming too," said Phyllis. She wasn't kidding.

"Are you getting married?" I asked.

"We may. I'm not sure," she replied.

From my mother's expression I could tell she wasn't wild about this Florida idea either.

"Where will you live?" I said. "This is your home."

Phyllis patted my hand. "It's time I had a place of my own, and now I can afford it. They have some lovely condos on the beach."

"Oh, Phyllis," I cried, rubbing my eyes.

"Don't be so melodramatic, Libby," said Dad, as he dribbled molasses over his stack of pancakes. "What Phyllis does is her business."

"But why Florida?" I continued. "You could buy your own house right here!"

"Boston has many fine attributes. Climate is not one of them," Phyllis replied.

"How about skin cancer? You always say too much sun is bad for you." I had her now.

"It takes more years for skin cancer to develop than I've got left. I've been careful all my life. Now I can splurge."

I glanced at my parents. "Can we go, too?"

"Your father and I have work here," my mother said.

"But what about me? Doesn't anybody care how I feel about this?"

They all looked at each other.

"This is Phyllis's chance to have a life of her own," said my mother, after a long silence. "It's a wonderful opportunity. She deserves it."

She made it sound as though living with us had been worse than hard labor in Siberia.

"I like things the way they are. I don't want it to change," I said.

"You can't fight the inevitable, Lib," said Dad.

"What does *inevitable* mean?" I wiped the milk off my chin.

"Certain to happen," replied Phyllis. "As in 'Boston will get at least one twelve-inch snowstorm every winter.'"

"Or as in 'Phyllis will leave me.'"

Two

The Countdown

• "That's my forty-eighth." I pointed to the small, rusted, yellow car driving past.

"Darn! I wish I'd seen it first." Jess cracked her gum. "At this rate, I'll never beat you."

Jess and I sat on the stone wall in front of the library. We were Beetle-counting, and this was a prime location. In the three weeks since school started, I had counted fifteen Volkswagen Beetles passing here.

"If your grandmother would let you ride over to the rotary near Fresh Pond, I could hit fifty today," Jess said.

"She says there's too much traffic there."

"That's the point." Jess pushed up the sleeves of her sweatshirt. "Maybe after she moves to Florida we can."

"Why'd you have to bring that up?"

"Sorry, I wasn't thinking." Blowing a huge pink bubble, she jumped off the wall. "The way they whiz around that rotary, I bet we'd see ten in half an hour."

"Cut it out."

"Okay, okay." Keeping her eyes on the street, she leaned against the wall. "When does Phyllis take to the friendly skies?"

"Next weekend. She says she has to get her affairs in order first."

"Sounds like she's dying instead of moving."

"Yeah." I sighed.

"Best thing for you is to get your mind on something else." Jess cleared her throat. "Now, the way I figure it, you'll hit fifty by Monday, so we'd better plan a strategy for getting Ben to talk to you."

Jess is an expert at strategies. I'm not sure if she loves it because she's good at it, or the other way around. She can beat anyone in our school — including teachers — at chess, Stratego, and Go. Once she even beat the president of the Upper School Chess Club.

I'm glad she has plenty of experience, because getting Ben Tweitelbaum to be the first boy who talks to me after I count fifty Beetles isn't going to be easy.

"Are you positive you want it to be him?"

I nodded. It *had* to be Ben.

With a pinky finger, Jess twisted one of her tight, reddish-brown curls. "You realize he's been known to go weeks without speaking to a girl."

"He's shy sometimes."

Jess wrinkled her nose. She isn't too interested in boys. In fact, she was only counting Beetles for the challenge of hitting fifty before I did. She says it's stupid to think the first boy who talks to you after you see your fiftieth one will become your husband. I know that. But it's still fun to think about marrying Ben.

"This requires clever scheming, Libby. I'll have to think about it more."

"Forty-nine!" I shouted, as a bright orange Beetle turned at the light.

"Let's count Cadillacs next time. Beetles are too easy." She grabbed my arm. "Come down from there and don't look at any more cars."

"Why not?" I hopped off the wall.

"It's too soon." She spun me around so my back was to the street. "Step one of the plan: You must see Beetle Number Fifty when the probability of being near Ben is highest. Otherwise, some other turkey might talk to you first."

It seemed logical.

"Go home the back way, and if you hear a car coming, keep your eyes on the ground."

"I'll hit something."

"No, you won't. I'll call you tomorrow after my father brings me back from Ipswich and tell you the rest of the plan."

I picked my bike off the grass and aimed it toward Elm Street. "If it's your day with him, how will you have time to think of a plan?"

"Come on, Libby. You know him." She paused to blow a bubble. "I'll have mucho time."

Somehow I made it home without plowing into a tree every time a car passed. I decided it wasn't safe to use my bike again until after I reached fifty.

Grabbing an apple from the fruit dish, I stopped to see Samantha and George. When they spotted the apple, they went crazy. Squeal, squeal! It sounded like the civil defense test on the radio. In stereo.

As I lifted the lid, they rested their front paws on the side of the cage and stuck their mouths up in the air.

"Here you go, tubby." I bit off a chunk of apple and held it out to George. He snatched it with his teeth and, like a flash, ran to the back corner. Samantha was more polite. She nibbled hers while I held it. I gave her a second chunk, then closed the lid.

As I passed the living room, I saw Dad in the recliner with a book in his lap. He was staring at the wall, probably picturing an equation sprawled from the front door to the fireplace.

"Hi, Dad."

He jerked around in his chair. "Oh, Lib. I didn't hear you come in. I was toying with an idea for a minute."

"Thought so."

"How about a game of Mastermind when I finish this chapter?"

"Sure." I headed back through the kitchen toward the stairs.

The study door was open. My mother sat at the desk, which was covered with law books and folders. Although her back was to the door, I could see she was writing on a yellow legal pad.

We have a special door signal at our house. If you don't mind an interruption, you leave the door open. But I didn't dare go into my mother's study. I knew she didn't want to be bothered. She had only left the door open so she wouldn't feel guilty about working on Saturday.

She wore a pair of white pants and a purple turtle-neck with a scarf at her neck. My mother always looks perfect, even on weekends.

Her name fits her. Graceful. Dignified. I bet if you saw her on the street, you'd say, "That woman's name must be Anne." No one ever calls her Annie. She's not the kind of person you give a nickname. She's also not the kind of mother you call Mommy or Mom.

I think names are very important. Maybe names even make people act the way they do. Jess, for example. That name could be short for Jessica, a girl, or Jesse, a boy. But Jess's parents named her plain old Jess, so nobody can be sure.

When Jess started our school in the middle of last year, our fifth-grade teacher was confused about whether she was a girl or boy. Since she keeps her hair short and wears jeans and sweatshirts, you couldn't blame the teacher. Jess thought it was hilarious when she got yelled at for going in the girls' bathroom. Phyllis says all that will change as soon as Jess's hormones take over.

Once I asked Phyllis about my name. "I'd rather be called Elizabeth," I said. "It's more impressive and romantic. Like a queen."

Phyllis laughed. "Honey, you're a Libby. Elizabeth

would fit you about as well as your father's winter boots."

Or my mother's high heels.

I started upstairs. The first step creaked. I glanced back toward the study. But my mother didn't turn around.

Phyllis's winter clothes were scattered around her room. Stepping over a pile of wool skirts, I flopped down on her bed.

"Hit fifty yet?" she asked.

"Almost. Probably by Monday."

She tossed an armful of coats onto her pink flowered chair. "It's about time I weeded my closet. I never realized how much I've accumulated since I moved in here."

That was after my grandfather died. I was two.

"I won't need warm clothes anymore." She peered at me over the tops of her bifocals. "Except when I visit you."

"What are you going to do with everything?"

"Most goes to the Senior Citizens' rummage sale. Anne might want a few things." She reached into a box sitting on the closet floor and handed me a red felt hat with a black pom-pom on top. It smelled of moth crystals. "Would you like this?"

I examined the round, flat hat. It *was* unusual.

"It's a Scottish tam. Try it on."

Awkwardly, I fitted the hat on my head.

"No, no," Phyllis said. "Tilt it to one side. That's it. You look very stylish."

Stylish for what century?

"When you wear it, think of me." She quickly stuck her head in the closet, but not before I saw her eyes watering.

I lay back on the pillow and stared at the ceiling. I liked the way the lines in the wallpaper pattern danced if I looked at them long enough. It reminded me of how a cobweb vibrates when the spider walks across it.

Phyllis's comforter felt soft against my skin. I would miss lounging on her bed. I could still come and gaze at the ceiling, but it wouldn't be the same. And the comforter would be gone.

"Are you sure you want to go through with this, Phyllis?" The wallpaper lines were jumping.

"Yes," was the muffled reply from inside the closet.

"Why do you have to leave so soon? Couldn't you wait a few months?" Or years.

"Once the decision is made, there's no reason to wait around. Besides, it's better to go before the winter people arrive and snatch up all the nice condominiums."

"Who will take care of me? They're so busy."

"Don't underestimate your parents, Libby." She stepped out into the room. "I suspect they'll rise to the occasion once I'm out of the picture."

"And what if they don't?"

"You'll manage fine without me. After all, you're eleven going on forty."

"What does that mean?"

"It means I wouldn't go if I didn't think you were old enough." She sat on the bed and stroked my hair. "It's hard for me to leave you, sweetie. But in the long run, it's best for both of us — and for Anne and Rod, too. In a few years you won't need me. But Mr. S. will, and I like to be needed. You understand, don't you?"

Closing my eyes, I nodded. What else could I do?

Half the time, grownups expect you to act like an adult, because they say you're old enough to understand. The other half, they *don't* want you to act like an adult, because they say you're too young to understand.

Why can't they make up their minds?

Three

Beetle #50

• Violet Van picks me up every morning at the corner of Washington and School streets. Eight of us ride Violet. A third- and fourth-grader get on downtown. Three kids are picked up at Common Street. Then Violet swings by our corner to meet Meghan Drake, who's a fifth-grader, and me.

I almost forgot (I wish I could forget!) Candace Stewart, our last stop. There's only one thing wrong with riding Violet Van, and that's Candace.

The reason I don't walk like other kids in my neighborhood is because I go to a private school. My parents are fanatics about my education.

I used to take the MBTA to Cambridge, then walk a couple of blocks to my school. But two years ago Todd Hasselheim nearly got snatched on his way from the bus stop, when a guy jumped out of the

BEETLE #50 • 21

bushes. Todd kicked him in the right place and ran. The next week a bunch of Belmont parents hired a van to drive us.

"I heard your grandmother won the lottery," Meghan called, as I approached the corner. She was balanced on one foot on top of the fire hydrant. Meghan wants to be a gymnast. Any object under five inches in diameter is a challenge. "A million dollars! That's great."

"I guess so."

"I wish someone in my family would win the lottery. You're lucky."

Lucky. That's me. "Here comes Violet."

Meghan hopped off the hydrant and gathered her books.

"Morning." Our driver Nora smiled as we climbed aboard.

Today Violet Van smelled like lilies. "Funeral over the weekend, Nora?" I asked.

"Right again," she replied. "We had two dozen lily plants and five memorial wreaths. Busy day."

I've developed a good nose for flowers in the past two years. Nora and her husband are florists. When it isn't carting us around, Violet Van is their delivery truck. How many kids get delivered to school by FTD?

When Nora first started driving, Violet was an ordinary white van with THE FLOWER BASKET printed on its door. One day the back was filled with African violets that she planned to drop off later. So Meghan and I called it Violet Van.

"Dull and idiotic," Candace said, when she heard our name.

The next week Nora painted VIOLET VAN across the front in purple letters. She says our name gives the van character. So *there*, Candace.

I picked up a tiny card under my foot.

"What's it say?" Meghan asked.

" 'With deepest sympathy on your loss.' Must have dropped off one of the memorial wreaths."

"Aren't we picking up Candace?" someone up front said, as Nora turned toward Cambridge.

"Her mother's taking her in this morning."

"No great loss," murmured Meghan.

I raised my eyes skyward. "A gift from the heavens."

Meghan took the card and laid it on Candace's seat. "May she rest in peace." She giggled. "Forever!"

"Amen."

Fred Chan, a second-grader, turned around and stared at us though his thick, round glasses. "The older you get, the weirder you get."

Meghan and I cracked up.

Soon Nora pulled up at school. "Unless you have petals or roots, the ride's over."

Meghan and I, still giggling, were last off.

"Why are you two so gleeful this morning?" Nora's eyes twinkled.

"It's our morning mourning," I replied, laughing. Then stuffing the card into my jacket pocket, I hurried in the front gate.

Jess was already at our meeting place — the forsythia bush under the science room window. She lives in Cambridge and walks to school.

"I like your new look," I said. She had on a turquoise warm-up suit with matching pants and shirt. "But it definitely changes your image."

"Ha ha." Jess rolled her eyes.

"Which one bought it for you?"

"The father. Can't wait to see what the mother gets to beat it. I made sure she saw the price tag this morning."

"How come you didn't call me yesterday about the plan?"

"Got home too late."

"You thought of a plan, didn't you?"

"Well, not quite."

"Jess!" I shrieked. The kids on the climbing gym stared at me. "What will I do if I hit fifty today?"

She patted my shoulder, then popped a bubble in my face.

"Ouch." I rubbed my ear.

"Don't worry. I'll come up with something."

Before I could strangle her, Mr. Ashley, our headmaster, appeared on the front steps with the bell. When I first came here, I was impressed by that bell. It's the brass kind with a straight black handle like the ones they had in one-room schoolhouses. A third-grader rings it every day. I used to try to be first in line so I'd be picked.

"Fourth grade first in today," announced Mr. Ashley. The fourth grade cheered, proud of themselves for lining up before the other classes.

Sixth grade was last, as usual. We don't plan to line up fast until January, or maybe December if it's a cold winter.

Jess and I shuffled through the front door into the hall. The building looks more like a big house than a school. In fact, it *was* a house a hundred years ago when two ladies started classes. Then it was only for girls. Thank goodness that changed.

Each classroom has a fireplace (but we don't use them), a cloakroom, and wide window seats. Miss Harper lets us sit on them during quiet reading.

Even though it's a private school, most kids aren't rich or snobby. Many are on scholarship. Kids from towns all around Boston come here. The brochure calls it "a diverse student body." Imagine a student with a diverse body. Arms from Watertown, head from Brookline, legs from Somerville.

For some reason, my parents liked the idea of a diverse body. They were also sold by the small classes and the "bright and dedicated" teachers. Of course, they hadn't met Gross Ed, my math teacher, yet.

When I walked into the cloakroom, Candace Stewart was standing directly in front of my hook. "Miss Harper says my history display is outstanding," she said loudly. "My mother helped me bring it today."

"Could you move?"

She didn't budge. "I was the first to complete the

assignment. I bet some people haven't even started."

I reached over her head and tossed my lunch bag into the cubby.

"Now I'm going to start an extra credit project," Candace continued.

Out of the corner of my eye, I noticed a white blob on the bottom of my lunch bag. The yoghurt was leaking. And the blob was about to drop right on Candace's gorgeous blonde tresses. "You better move, Candace."

She shot me her drop-dead-moron look.

Don't say I didn't warn you, I thought.

"Doesn't anyone want to know who my famous ancestor is?"

"I know!" said Natalie.

"Of course you do, stupid. I told you. I was talking to everyone else."

"Oh." Natalie lowered her eyes.

Kerplunk! The blob fell. Bull's eye. It landed on the barrette clipped at the back of Candace's head. She didn't seem to feel it.

"Let me guess," said Jess. "The Plymouth Rock now rests in our classroom." She stuck her nose up in the air and strutted around the cloakroom. Her imitation of Candace was perfect.

"Actually, I probably *do* have Mayflower ancestors." Candace tossed her head, and the yoghurt dripped into her hair. Yuck! "However, my project is about Daniel Boone."

"You mean they let someone who wore a coonskin cap in *your* family?" said Jess.

"You're thinking of Davy Crockett. Daniel Boone never wore coonskin, only felt hats."

"And designer jeans, too, right?" Jess snickered and strutted some more.

Most of the kids in the cloakroom burst out laughing.

Candace's face turned the color of a ripe tomato. "I'll get you for this," she hissed. "Let's go, Natalie." She stomped out.

"I'm shakin' in my sneakers," Jess called after her.

"I hope she doesn't realize how that yoghurt got in her hair."

"What?" asked Jess.

"Never mind." I opened my bag and tightened the yoghurt container. "Why do you try to get her mad at you? Everyone knows you shouldn't mess with Candace."

"I'm not afraid of her," she replied. "She makes me so sick, I have to say something."

I'd warned Jess the first day she arrived here last year to watch her step with Candace. Jess never listened. Maybe it's because she hasn't seen what Candace does to her enemies.

Like what she did to the girl who accidentally spilled orange paint on Candace's snow scene and then made the mistake of laughing about it. After Candace got through with her, they had to cut off the girl's braids.

Or how she got even with the boy who wouldn't let her cheat off his math quiz. Candace called the missing kid hotline and said she recognized the boy's face on a milk carton. It took his grandparents, with whom he lived, two weeks to convince police from three states that the picture wasn't the boy's and that he wasn't missing or kidnapped.

The worst part was that Candace *never* got caught. Even when it was obvious — to us kids, anyway — that she was the culprit, there never was any hard evidence to prove it. So, Candace continued to take revenge on anyone who crossed her, while appearing as innocent as an angel.

As I hung up my jacket, Tricia Chittendom tapped my shoulder. "I saw your grandmother on TV. What's she going to do with all her money?"

"Move to Florida."

"I bet you'll go down every winter vacation and get a great tan. Lucky you."

"She's the eightieth person to tell me I'm lucky," I said when Tricia left. "Why does everybody say that?"

Jess shrugged. "It's exciting."

"Not for me. I wish they'd all shut up about it."

As soon as I'd checked that Ben was in school, I started searching for Beetles. During quiet reading I claimed one of the window seats. Although I could see a block in both directions, no Beetles appeared.

Gross Ed's room faces the playground, so I had to stop the Beetle-watch during math. I didn't mind, since Ben sits in front of me. I get to stare at him all period, without Ben knowing.

Ben's hands are his best feature. The veins stand out on the back, and his fingers are long and slender. They got that way from playing the flute. I know because I asked him one time when I was feeling brave and he wasn't feeling shy.

I used to think the flute was a girl's instrument. All the other boys I know play trombones or drums. But Ben never gets teased, because everyone respects him.

"He's a natural-born leader," Phyllis told me when

she helped with *Peter Pan* last year. Ben was stage manager. "You have impeccable taste in men, Libby."

I know.

Jess ran up to me after math class. "The plan's in motion," she whispered. "Tell me when you hit fifty."

"What *is* the plan?"

"Uh oh." She grabbed my arm and pulled me up the stairs to the cafeteria. "Get your milk fast. Here comes Arthur."

Climbing two steps at a time, I made my escape.

Arthur has been chasing me since third grade. If you think I'm bragging, you haven't met Arthur. He expresses his love like men who give candy and flowers. Only Arthur does it with dairy products. Every lunch he tries to buy my chocolate milk. Last Valentine's Day he brought his mother's blender to school and mixed me a strawberry milkshake. The kid is very strange.

"Whew, made it," I said, when Jess and I were safely outside by our forsythia bush.

"He's getting tricky. He almost caught you today. Maybe you should tell him you're allergic to milk."

"He'd only try something else. I hate to think what it might be."

"True. Arthur is capable of anything."

I walked to the trash can to toss my apple core. That's when I saw it. "Beetle Number Fifty! There, at the corner."

Jess ran over. She shoved a pencil into my hand. "Find Ben fast."

"What's the pencil for?"

"The plan, Libby. I borrowed it from him in math. And you're going to return it right now. He's so polite, he'll —"

"He'll say thank you!" Jess's strategy was brilliant.

I spotted him on the back playground kicking a soccer ball.

"Hurry," she said, "and don't talk to anyone."

Keeping my eyes glued on Ben, I jogged toward him. My heart pounded. My fingers gripped the pencil. Close to the playground gate, I broke into a run.

Crash!

The next thing I knew, I was sprawled on the ground. Ben's pencil lay broken in my hand. A piece of graphite stuck in my thumb.

On the grass beside me sat Arthur. "Somehow we collided, Libby."

"Aaugh!" I screamed. "Don't you dare say another word to me. Ever!"

I dug into my pocket for a tissue to wipe the blood from my thumb. All I found was the card, "With deepest sympathy on your loss." And what a loss it was!

Arthur leaned closer. "Congratulations on your grandmother winning the lottery."

Slapping my hands over my ears, I jumped up and dashed for the forsythia bush at sixty miles per hour. Three weeks of counting Beetles and what do I get? Arthur.

Four

Nobody Home

• "Start counting again," Meghan said, when I told her how Arthur had ruined everything. "Ben can be your second husband."

I hadn't thought of that. "Maybe I can get rid of Arthur by poisoning his milkshakes."

"Or divorce him. Your mother could get you lots of alimony."

"She's not that kind of lawyer. Besides, I'd rather knock him off."

I counted a dozen Beetles before giving up. It wasn't fun the second time around. And I was afraid something would go wrong again, and I'd end up with someone even worse than Arthur — if that was possible. I couldn't handle any more disappointment for a while. Phyllis's leaving was enough.

My parents forced me to go to the airport the night

Phyllis left. I didn't want to go. I wanted to kiss her good night before I went to bed, the way I always did. Then, by the time I awoke the next morning, Phyllis would already have arrived in Florida. It would have been better that way.

But they made me say goodbye at the airport. I try not to think about it. Yet every time I close my eyes, I see Phyllis walking away from me. She headed through that tunnel to her plane, her arm linked with Mr. S.'s. Then they passed a curve in the tunnel, and Phyllis disappeared.

Before she'd been gone a week, I knew that her winning the lottery was the worst thing that ever happened to me. Nothing was the same. Not even our phone number.

After the TV interview, the phone rang an average of seven times an hour (Dad figured it out) from 8:00 A.M. until midnight. Investment experts, salesmen, real estate agents. Phyllis called them society's leeches. She told them she and Mr. S. were only getting $40,000 a year and weren't really millionaires. They kept calling anyway. It didn't stop even after Phyllis left, so my mother got us a new number.

She also got us Mrs. Gould.

Mrs. Gould comes two days a week. Having her around is like having termites. You never see her, but you know she's been there.

She cleans the house, changes sheets, washes clothes, shops for groceries, cooks and freezes all our dinners, and is gone before I get home from school My mother thinks she's great. I'd like to call the exterminator.

I used to look forward to coming home every afternoon. That's changed too. When Phyllis was here, we baked cookies or watched her soaps. If I wanted to be by myself, I went upstairs to read comics or do homework. But now nobody's home when I get there. I found out that being alone is different from being by myself.

On Tuesday afternoon, the ten-day anniversary of Phyllis's leaving, Violet Van dropped me off earlier than usual. After making sure no one was watching, I picked up the fake rock sitting along the edge of our front walk. Inside was the house key. Supposedly, no burglar will know that one of the twenty rocks is plastic. But it seems to me it's a burglar's business to spot fake rocks.

I gathered up the mail scattered on the floor under

the slot. Nothing interesting. No letter from Phyllis. No *TV Guide*. No free samples.

Everything was quiet except for the hum of the refrigerator. That was a good sign. On the other hand, maybe not. Burglars are very quiet.

Gripping Dad's umbrella with the sharp point, I began my rounds. First the hall closet. I checked the floor. No feet there. Then the living room, kitchen, back hall, study. All clear. Upstairs next. I looked under the beds and in the closets. Carefully, I pulled aside the shower curtain. Satisfied that I was completely alone in the house, I put the umbrella back in its ceramic stand near the front door.

"Chirp. Chirp." The phone thinks it's a cricket. My mother bought it because she says the chirp is less obtrusive than ordinary phone bells.

Well, it obtruded on me. In fact, it nearly gave me a heart attack. My hands were still shaking when I picked up the receiver.

"Hello."

"May I speak to your mother?" A man's voice.

"Uh, she's busy at the moment. Can I take a message?" I'm supposed to lie when I'm alone.

"Maybe your father could help me."

The guy started to worry me. He wouldn't give up.

"He's in the shower." I tried to imagine the sound of water running in the bathroom so I'd be more convincing.

"I understand," he said.

I hope you don't, I thought.

"Please tell them Bud Thompson called."

Relief. I'd heard the name before. Their insurance agent or something.

"I'll tell them. Goodbye."

The phone call reminded me that I hadn't checked in. I dialed my mother's office. Sara, her secretary, answered.

"This is Libby Pruitt. May I speak to my mother?"

"I'm sorry, Libby. She's in court."

"Will you tell her I'm home?"

"Of course."

I don't know why she wants me to call. She's never there anyway. I wonder what would happen if I got kidnapped on the way home.

"Call your parents and get the ransom, or it's curtains, kid," the kidnapper would growl.

I'd call my father's office first. There'd be no answer because he was lecturing or, more likely, because he was tuned out.

Then I'd try my mother. "Your mother is in an important meeting and can't be disturbed," Sara would say.

"But I'm being held captive."

"One minute please." Click. She'd put me on hold. Violin music would play. I'd hear the themes from *The Sound of Music* and *M.A.S.H.* and four other songs I didn't recognize.

Finally, Sara would come back on. "Still holding? Good, I'll be with you in a moment."

Click. I'm disconnected.

"Let me call back," I'd plead with the kidnapper. But he'd be tired of waiting. "Any last wishes, kid?"

I poured myself a glass of milk and grabbed a carrot from the refrigerator. Out on the porch George and Samantha squealed.

"Here you go, George." I lifted him from the cage and gave him half the carrot. Dragging it with his teeth, he ran under the lounge chair.

Samantha sat in my lap and nibbled hers. I stroked her blonde fur. She made a purring noise — at least as close to a purr as guinea pigs get. That's when I felt the twitch in her tummy. I gently moved my fingers around her middle. She was pregnant again. I could feel three babies.

When I named George after George Washington, I knew what I was doing. He may not be Father of his Country yet, but he's working on it. Samantha has already had eight litters.

While George and Samantha ran around the porch, I rolled up the dirty newspaper in the bottom of their cage. I put fresh paper and cedar chips down and brought Samantha a dish of milk. Then I lay on the floor and let them climb over my legs. After a while, they both stretched out on my stomach and fell asleep.

It was almost dark when I heard my parents come in. "Hi, Lib." My dad kissed my forehead. "Have a good day?"

I sat on the bottom stair and watched them remove their coats. "It was okay."

"How'd you do on the math quiz?"

"I remembered to move all the decimal points the way you showed me."

"I hope you put the key back in the rock, Libby." My mother placed her coat on the hanger.

"Yes. Oh, a guy named Bud Thompson called."

"Rod, you were supposed to call him days ago."

"I guess it slipped my mind."

Things like calling insurance agents or buying a gallon of milk become very slippery in Dad's brain. But give him a mathematical formula, and he has the memory of a computer.

I followed them into the kitchen. My mother took a dish from the freezer. "Spinach lasagna sound good? Mrs. Gould says it's one of her specialties."

"Mrs. Gould says *every* meal is one of her specialties." Dad winked at me.

"She hasn't been wrong yet. We'll give it a try. You set the microwave, Rod, while I make the salad. Libby, the table, please."

She zipped around the kitchen from refrigerator to cupboard to sink. She made me nervous. I got the silverware and ducked out of her way.

Dad fiddled with the microwave controls. For a man who's so smart, he's really dumb about anything mechanical. He even has trouble setting stations on our car radio.

Once my mother told me that she had wanted a tape recording of me being born, with the first cry and all that. Dad was supposed to turn on the tape recorder when the doctor said I was coming out.

Later, they discovered he pushed the wrong button. She should never have trusted him with such an important job.

"Why do they make these things so complicated?" He scratched his head.

"Oh, Rod," my mother said impatiently. She pushed him aside and set it herself.

"We shouldn't have bought the microwave in the first place," I said. "The radiation might make me sterile."

"Where did you get that idea?" my mother asked.

"Phyllis read an article about it."

"I should have known," she said under her breath.

"I heard a story about it on TV, too."

"I think it's perfectly safe. And we have no choice. I can't possibly get dinner prepared before seven with an ordinary oven."

It'll be your fault if I can't have kids, I thought. But I didn't say any more about it.

They spent most of the meal talking about one of my mother's cases.

"What's *habeas corpus* mean?" I asked, trying to get in the conversation.

"Literally, 'to have a body,' " she said.

"Like a dead body?"

"Libby, I'm trying to discuss something with your father. Please don't keep interrupting."

I could take a hint. I concentrated on eating. The salad was okay, but Mrs. Gould's lasagna was over-rated. I finished my portion only because I was starved.

It wasn't until dessert that they got tired of discussing bodies. "Guess what?" I said, as Dad scooped the ice cream. "Samantha's pregnant again."

"That George is a little devil." He snickered.

"Three this time, I think. Isn't that great, Mother?"

"What are you going to do with them?"

"I have a waiting list. Jess wants one this time, too."

"Hmm." She rinsed off a plate and put it in the dishwasher.

"Can we bake a cake to celebrate? Phyllis and I always used to."

"You know where the cake mix is," she replied.

That wasn't exactly the response I was hoping for. I didn't want it to be a solo project. "I guess I won't bother."

"Here you go." Dad handed me a dish of mint chocolate chip sprinkled with cashews. "Sure you don't want some, Anne?"

"Not tonight." She wiped the counter next to the

microwave. "Don't forget to make your lunch before you go to bed, Libby."

"I'm out of Marshmallow Fluff. I need it for my peanut butter sandwich. Why didn't Mrs. Gould buy more?"

"She buys what I put on the list."

"Did you forget?"

"No."

"Can you ask her to get some this week?"

"It's not good for you."

"Phyllis said it was all right if I only had it with peanut butter. I don't use that much."

"Phyllis is not here anymore." It was the first time I had heard her courtroom voice at home since a TV repairman charged seventy-five dollars for telling us our set couldn't be fixed. "I choose our foods now, and I think it has too much sugar. It sticks to your teeth."

"But there's no good stuff for lunches around here."

"Then buy your lunch." I didn't like her expression.

"I'd have to sit in the cafeteria with the hot lunchers. All my friends are baggers."

"You'll have to make a choice. You're old enough to handle decisions on your own." She stalked out of the kitchen.

"What did I say wrong, Dad?"

He shook his head. "She's been under a lot of pressure since Phyllis left. I'm afraid I haven't been much help."

"But Mrs. Gould does everything."

"It's more than that, Lib." He gave me a hug. "I'd better go talk to her."

I finished my ice cream alone.

Peanut butter sandwiches without Fluff are pretty sickening. I was willing to try jelly, but we're out of that too. Permanently.

"Why don't you eat bologna or leftover chicken?" asked Jess, as we ate lunch in one of Miss Harper's window seats. It was too cold to be out by our forsythia bush.

"I'm not wild about meat."

"Then make a lettuce, tomato, and cheese sandwich."

"Too much work."

"Leave out the lettuce and tomato."

"Too dry."

"What's wrong with yoghurt?"

"According to my mother, not enough nutrition. It's like drinking a glass of milk."

Jess moaned. "I give up."

Across the room Natalie had her radio tuned to a rock station. With my fingernail, I tapped out the beat on the window pane. "Can I come home with you today?"

Jess crumpled her paperbag and shot it into the waste can. Miss Harper looked up when the can rattled.

"Well?"

"I told you *last* week. Wednesdays my mom has an aerobics class at the house."

"Want to go to Harvard Square and take the bus home?" I said.

"I thought they didn't like you hanging around there."

"Nobody will know."

"Aren't you supposed to call in?"

Jess was worse than my mother.

"Since when have you worried about following rules? I'll call after we get there. I'll only talk to the secretary anyway, so it doesn't matter."

"Oh yeah?" Jess cocked her head.

"Look," I said. "I don't want to go home right after school, okay?"

"Okay, okay. Don't get bent out of shape about it."

* * *

Harvard Square was just a few blocks from school, but they were *very* long blocks. "I should have left my looseleaf at school. My back is killing me." I swung the backpack off my shoulders and carried it in my arms.

"This was your idea, remember." Jess popped a bubble with her finger.

"There's a pay phone. I'll call my mother's office. Then let's get some ice cream."

Maybe a cold, damp October day isn't exactly ice cream weather, but I'd eat ice cream at thirty below. We got double dips and walked up by The Coop. The sidewalks were crowded with college students.

"Libby," said Jess, as we peered in the store windows. "You know I don't usually pay attention to clothes, but why have you started wearing that strange hat?"

"It's called a tam," I replied, touching the little pom-pom. "Unusual, isn't it?"

"It looks like you have a red Frisbee on your head."

"So what if it isn't the most attractive hat ever created? Phyllis gave it to me before she left. She'd be hurt if I didn't wear it."

Jess bit the bottom off her cone. "How's she going to know whether you wear it or not?"

"Maybe she'll ask. I'd feel bad lying to her. Besides, I like it." Well, not exactly. What I liked was the feeling I had when I wore it. As if Phyllis were here instead of a couple thousand miles away. But I didn't want to tell Jess that.

She shrugged. "It's your head. Put anything on it you want."

"Hey, look." I pointed to an oversized TV screen in the window of a video rental store across the street. "Want to see a free movie?"

Dodging traffic, we ran over. "Looks like a skin flick to me." Jess wrinkled her nose. "Must be triple-X-rated, at least."

"Do normal people do that stuff?"

"How should I know?"

A man inside banged on the window. Frowning, he turned off the set and motioned for us to move on.

"If he didn't want people watching, he shouldn't have it in his stupid window," Jess fumed.

"I don't care. It was disgusting anyway."

We went into a drugstore and I bought the new Spider-man comic. Jess got a T-shirt with a woman saying "Nuclear war! What about my career?" and a guy replying "You can get another job, darling."

I don't know why she wants to remind herself of that every time she looks in her drawer. I just hope she doesn't wear the shirt around me. I have enough to worry about.

At 4:45 we caught the bus for home. Since it was rush hour, we had to stand. Every time the bus hit a bump, a woman jabbed me in the kidneys with her elbow. The guy in back of me had garlic breath. I almost gagged when he exhaled.

Jess got off near her house. After fifteen minutes and stops at every corner, we arrived in Belmont. By then the sky was gray and the street lights were on. The tree limbs swaying in the wind looked like huge, black skeleton arms. I hurried home.

No lights in our windows. For a second I was glad. My parents wouldn't know I'd been gone. But then I got that quivery feeling in my stomach. It was dark behind those curtains. And empty.

As I picked up the fake rock, I heard strange honking above me. In the sky a flock of geese flew in a V-shape, going south for the winter. Just like Phyllis.

I unlocked the door and put the key back inside the hollow rock. When I looked again, the flock was out of sight. Then I noticed a single goose flying the wrong way.

He's searching for the flock, I thought. Maybe he's a young goose on his first migration. Now he's lost and all alone. He'll probably never find the others.

That one goose seemed to honk as loudly as the entire flock had. It was a sad honk. I could tell. I knew how he felt.

• Five

Mealworm Rendezvous

• For the past week we've studied mealworms in science class. We didn't see the real thing right away, because Ms. Reinholt's shipment from the supply company hadn't arrived. But we'd looked at pictures and learned all the parts.

Thursday we had a contest to see who knew the parts the best. Jess won. No surprise to me, but Candace was sure burned up about it.

"Maxilla wasn't on the worksheet," she said, pouting. "How was I supposed to know it was a mouth part?"

"We discussed it in class," replied Ms. Reinholt. I like her, because she's one of the few teachers who sees Candace for what she really is.

"No, we didn't. Did we, Natalie?"

"Uh, no. At least I don't think so."

"Perhaps if you both listened more carefully, you would have heard it." Ms. Reinholt turned to erase the blackboard.

"I hate her," Candace fumed. "Wait until my mother hears about this. She'll get the witch fired."

Fired? Are you kidding? They should give her a raise for shutting you up, I thought. But of course, I didn't say that to Candace.

On Monday Ms. Reinholt was still on the job. A glass cookie jar partly filled with oatmeal sat on the counter. Arthur already had his nose against the side of the jar.

"Hey, Ms. Reinholt. We gonna make breakfast? Ha, ha."

That Arthur is a real comedian.

"No, Arthur," she replied, as she placed fifteen baby-food jars next to the cookie jar. "Your mealworms have arrived. The oatmeal serves as food and a home for them. Today everyone will get three mealworms to care for."

"Oh joy," Candace muttered. "Just what I always wanted."

"Can I take one home for my pet chameleon?" Arthur stuck his hand in the jar.

Shaking her head, Ms. Reinholt grasped his wrist and pulled it out. Then she gently removed a mealworm and passed it around for us to see.

The mealworm was golden brown with six tiny legs near the front. I was surprised by the small size. The pictures and drawings had given me the idea that it was as long as an earthworm. Actually, it was only about twice the width of my thumb nail. It tickled when it walked across my hand. I couldn't wait to get my own.

"The mealworm isn't a worm at all. It's the larva of a common insect," said Ms. Reinholt. "Does anyone know which one?"

A hand went up across the room. It was Ben. He had on my favorite blue shirt. His brown hair was slightly mussed, the way I like it. It curled at the top of his collar. He'd probably get it cut soon. He always got a haircut when it hit the collar of the blue shirt.

"How repugnant!" shrieked Candace.

" 'Repugnant' she says," Jess whispered. "What a show-off!"

"What's repugnant?" Somewhere between the blue shirt and hair on the collar, I'd missed Ben's answer.

"It was a vocabulary word last week, remember?

It means distasteful and offensive." Jess leaned closer. "You want to know who's repugnant?" She pointed at Candace.

"I mean, what does the mealworm turn into?"

"A grain beetle. Where have you been?"

Dreamily, I gazed across the room.

"Libby." Ms. Reinholt said my name louder than usual.

"Yes?"

"Would you help distribute the jars?"

While I scooped oatmeal from a cereal box into the baby-food jars, she stuck labels on them. One by one, kids came up to get theirs.

"Put your name on the label. When you're ready, you may pick out your mealworms."

"There aren't enough jars, Ms. Reinholt. I didn't get one," I said.

"There's one at your seat. A friend must have taken it for you."

Jess stood in line at the cookie jar. "Thanks for getting mine," I said to her.

"Wasn't me." She raised her eyebrows.

Back at my seat I picked up the jar. Talk about repugnant! My name was written on the label in red ink surrounded with small red hearts and flowers. In a heart at the lower left corner, it said "L.P. + A.P.E. III." Only one person fit his initials to such perfection *and* was stupid enough to use them.

Arthur stared at me, waiting to see my reaction to his cute little gesture. I'd have shown him my honest reaction, but I liked Ms. Reinholt too much to barf all over her floor.

Hiding the label with my hand, I hurried to her desk. "Do you have any more labels? Mine got messed up."

She handed me a new one, then turned to the group at the cookie jar. "Take turns. No shoving."

I covered Arthur's handiwork and rewrote my name. By that time everyone had a magnifying glass and was getting to know the mealworms.

"Hurry and get yours," Jess said to me. "My larva challenges your larva to a race."

I guess it was because I was in a rush to join the fun that I made my big mistake. I spotted a mealworm buried in oatmeal near the bottom of the cookie jar. Without thinking, I plunged my hand in through the top and dug for him with my fingers. Too late I realized what I'd done.

Another hand — with veins that stood out on the back — rested against mine in the opening of the cookie jar.

"Uh, Libby, I think we have a problem." Ben looked at me with a half-smile. Considering the circumstances, it might have been a half-scowl, but I tried to have a positive attitude.

"Could you twist your wrist?" He pulled his hand up, but it ran into my thumb.

Turning my hand the other way, I tried to squeeze my thumb and fingers together. It didn't work. No doubt about it. Ben and I were stuck in the mouth of the cookie jar.

His fingers brushed against mine under the oatmeal. It was the closest I'd ever been to holding a boy's hand. "Why couldn't this have happened when I had fifty Beetles?" I murmured.

"If we don't get out of this soon, you *will* have fifty beetles," said Ben, "and they'll be crawling all over your fingers."

I hadn't thought of that. I wondered how long it took mealworms to change. "Do you think they're carnivorous? Some beetles eat flesh right off the bone."

"These only eat oatmeal. Now keep trying." He rotated his arm until our palms were together. "You push down while I pull up."

Still stuck.

By now Ms. Reinholt noticed something odd going on at her mealworm jar. "What in the world are you two doing?"

From the expression on Ben's face, I could tell he didn't plan to take the rap for this.

"I sort of stuck my hand in with Ben's," I whispered, so none of the kids would hear. "I guess the opening is narrower than I thought."

"Obviously." Ms. Reinholt half-scowled. It might have been a half-smile, but I wasn't feeling positive anymore.

The next thing I knew, the class was crowded around Ben and me. Most were giggling and cracking jokes. I noticed Ben wasn't laughing.

"You got in there. You certainly ought to be able to get out," Ms. Reinholt said with a worried voice.

"We've been trying," Ben said. "Believe me."

"How about soap?" someone suggested. "That works when rings get stuck."

So they soaped our wrists. It didn't help. Then Ms.

Reinholt decided to rub oil around the rim of the jar. All that did was to get Ben and me greasy.

"Once I got my finger stuck in an aspirin bottle," Arthur said. "They had to break the bottle. See, I still have the scar."

"You're a big help," I moaned.

The bell rang, signaling the end of the class period. Ms. Reinholt shooed everyone out the door.

"Good going, Libby," Candace sneered, as she passed. "A first-class act."

I wanted to tell her to put a clothespin on her lips. Of course, I didn't. Instead, I stuck my tongue out — at her back.

"You two stay here," Ms. Reinholt said. "I'm going to get Mr. Ashley."

"Where does she think we're going to go?" Ben chuckled. Maybe he wasn't too mad after all. "Let's move this jar down to a table. My arm's almost numb."

Holding the bottom, we carefully placed the jar on the nearest lab table. With his free hand, Ben pulled over two stools. "Have a seat. This might take a while."

I looked at the clock. We'd been attached for over

an hour. Already my conversation with Ben had exceeded all previous records. What if we stayed like this for the rest of the day? Think what it could do for our relationship.

Once I read about two artists who were tied together by a long rope for a year. They said they became *very* close friends.

Just as I was pondering the wonderful moments we could share, I realized I had to go to the bathroom. BAD. In all the excitement, I hadn't noticed it creeping up on me. Suddenly, being attached to Ben didn't seem so terrific anymore.

"They better do something quick!"

"Don't get upset, Libby. I was only kidding about the beetles."

"That's not what I'm worried about." I squeezed my legs together.

"Oh. You too?"

Our eyes met in a moment of mutual understanding.

Finally, Ms. Reinholt returned with Mr. Ashley and Ned, the custodian. Ned had a sharp knife.

"It's all right," Mr. Ashley assured us. "Ned had this glass cutter in the basement. It's the only way we can think of to get you loose."

Ben and I were in no position to argue.

"Sit still. Don't want to nick you." Ned started cutting.

I closed my eyes and concentrated on the path to the girls' room. In a few minutes I felt the oatmeal and mealworms fall away from my fingers.

"You're free now," Ms. Reinholt said. "Let me wash that grease off your —"

But before she could finish, Ben and I dashed out the door.

"Definitely the height of romanticism," Jess said, as we put on our coats at the end of the day. "I have to admit, I'd never have thought of getting stuck in a cookie jar as a way to attract a boy's attention. Very creative, Libby."

"Thanks. I thought you'd like it."

"No, I'm serious. You should send this in to *Seventeen*. 'How to snare a guy and hold on to him for six ninety-five.' Isn't that how much Mr. Ashley says you owe the school for the cookie jar?"

"He's such a grouch. Ms. Reinholt wouldn't have made me pay. It was an accident, after all." I picked up my backpack and headed for the gate. Violet Van hadn't arrived, so I leaned against the fence to wait.

"This one's better: 'Get the boy of your dreams to stick with you and have a larva-ly time.' "

"How long are you going to keep this up, Jess?"

At that moment Ben passed by on his bike. Waving, he called to me, " 'Bye, Libby. Watch what you do with your hands."

Jess's mouth dropped open. She was speechless, but only for a second. "That *was* our terribly shy Ben, wasn't it? I must have missed something."

I nodded.

"I get it. Shared adversity brought you closer. That's it, isn't it?"

"Something like that," I replied, smiling.

Six

One More Annoying Detail

• I wish shared adversity had the same effect on my mother that it did on Ben. Since Phyllis left, she's been in a lousy mood. I don't think she likes dealing with household details like grocery lists or broken washing machines or newspaper subscriptions or all the other things Phyllis used to handle.

I also don't think she's too keen about dealing with me.

If Dad hadn't been away for a few days at a meeting of math professors, I would have spared her the trouble of the $6.95 cookie jar. Such details don't bother him. He just ignores them. He'd have given me the money and forgotten about it — especially if I'd asked him for it while he was working on an equation.

Unfortunately, Mr. Ashley wanted the money right

away. I was forced to explain the entire episode to my mother.

"It was your error, Libby. You should use your own money to pay for the cookie jar." She picked a magazine off the floor and placed it on the coffee table.

I hadn't planned on bringing up the subject of my finances until her mood improved, but she gave me no choice. "Since Phyllis left, no one has remembered to give me my allowance. I'm broke."

"Why didn't you say something before?"

Allowances are another annoying detail. "I don't know."

"How much did Phyllis give you?"

When I told her, she hit the ceiling.

"That includes extra for mopping the back steps and dusting downstairs," I added quickly. I followed her into the kitchen where she filled the watering can.

"Since Mrs. Gould does that now, we'll go back to the original allowance. Enough to cover milk at school, bus fare home when you visit Jess, and a little extra for spending money."

"Little is right! That doesn't leave me enough to buy even one comic a week."

"Then maybe you should use the library. The books

are free," she replied, as she watered the spider plant in the front window.

"But I like comics. They have great stories."

"A girl with your ability should be reading fine literature, not simple-minded trash."

"They're not trash," I said angrily. "*Phyllis* says there's nothing wrong with them."

She spun around. Her cheeks were red, and it wasn't from her blusher, either. As she opened her mouth to speak, the phone chirped.

I made a break for it. Lucky for me, the call was an emergency case. She spent the rest of the evening in the study.

The next afternoon I was still trying to figure out how to get the $6.95. Jess didn't have enough to loan me, at least that's what she said. And I couldn't withdraw any from my bank account without my mother's signature.

I picked up the mail under the slot. There was a manila envelope for me postmarked Florida. I tore it open.

DEAR LIBBY,
   I saw the enclosed *Catwoman* comic when Mr. S.

and I went for the Sunday paper. It's an exciting issue. I read it on the beach this morning.

Even though this is hurricane season, the weather has been sunny and pleasant. I bought a new bathing suit yesterday. For a septuagenarian, I look darn good in it.

I enjoyed your letter. Congratulations for the A on your math quiz. The news about Samantha is wonderful. Will you call me the minute the babies are born?

Can't wait until you come down for a visit. We have plenty of room here.

Take care and give your Mother and Dad a hug from me.

XOXOXO
Love, Phyllis

I read it over ten times. It made me feel warm inside, as if Phyllis had her arm around me. But each time I reached the end, I felt lonely again. It was like standing in the middle of a vacant lot with my baseball glove when all the other kids had gone home for dinner.

I put the letter back in the envelope. It would take more than reading Phyllis's words to make things the way then used to be.

I wish my mother was more like Phyllis. She used to be fun when I was little. She'd take me places like the circus or movies. Then she started law school and everything changed.

She was never around anymore. Phyllis was the one who made cupcakes for my birthdays and took me to swimming lessons. When we had field trips, Phyllis helped chaperone. Some of the kids thought *she* was my mother.

My mother's idea of spending time with me was enrolling us in a dance class. She loved it, but I was a big flop. When it comes to being graceful, I'm more like a hippopotamus than a ballerina. I would have enjoyed just messing around with her. But I guess she thought that was too boring.

After I ate my snack and checked in with Sara the secretary, I went up to my room and read Catwoman's latest adventure. Phyllis was right about its being an exciting issue.

When I reached under my bed for the big cardboard box where I store my comic books, I didn't feel it. Pulling up the bedspread, I peeked under. No box.

I was sure I hadn't moved it. I *never* moved it. It had to be Mrs. Gould. I knew she had cleaned, because the dust balls under the bed were gone. She must have put it somewhere else.

I checked all the logical places. Closet, bookcase, desk. But no box. Two years of comic books were in it, including a few limited editions and fourteen collector's issues that Phyllis found for me in a second-hand bookstore. I could never replace some of them.

I tore the house apart. I even checked the storage closet and the attic. Frantically paging through the address book, I found Mrs. Gould's phone number. So what if her husband worked nights and didn't like to be disturbed during the day? The woman better tell me where my comics were.

I let the phone ring thirty times before giving up. As I put down the receiver, I glanced out the window. On the curb next to our garbage cans sat a black plastic bag. Trash pickup was the next morning. Mrs. Gould always put out the cans before she left.

I bolted outside and ripped open the black bag. "Aaugh!" I screamed, when I saw my comics. The box was torn and crushed, but the books seemed all right. What a relief!

That evening I greeted my mother with the evidence. "She had no right to throw out my belongings," I shouted.

"I'm sure it was unintentional." She put down her briefcase. "That old box *did* look rather ragged."

"What's she do around here — throw away anything that doesn't look brand new?"

"Calm down."

"Don't you care that she tried to destroy my property? She didn't even ask if it was important."

"Mrs. Gould is a big help. We should be grateful to have her."

"The next thing will be my looseleaf notebook, then my fuzzy throw rug. Who knows? She'll probably try to get rid of Samantha and George too." My eyes began to water.

"I refuse to discuss this when you're hysterical."

"I don't want Mrs. Gould here. We don't need her. Phyllis could run the house alone."

"Phyllis," she said in an ugly voice, "did not have a full-time job."

I hated her. I wanted her to feel as bad as I did. "I wish you had gone to Florida instead of Phyllis."

"Don't ever talk to me like that again!" The sting of her hand across my face shocked me. She had never hit me before. She didn't believe in it. I thought.

Tears streaming down my face, I ran to my room and slammed the door.

Later she knocked. She wanted to talk. I wouldn't open it. Let her feel guilty. Let her suffer.

Two nights later Dad and I were playing Mastermind while my mother was at a dinner meeting in Boston.

"I hear it was somewhat stormy while I was gone." He looked up from the gameboard. "And I don't mean the weather."

"Yeah, there were a couple of cloudbursts."

"Can I do anything?" he asked.

I knew it wouldn't help to complain to him about my allowance, or Mrs. Gould, or the $6.95 cookie jar. He always backed up my mother, no matter what. I shook my head.

He looked relieved.

Seven

Going into Business

• The good news is Mr. Ashley has the $6.95 for the cookie jar. The bad news is my mother loaned me the money to pay him, so I'm still in debt.

"The way I see it," Jess said, "there's only one reasonable strategy for solving your problem. Go into business."

We sat cross-legged on the floor of her room. We'd been sitting that way for a half hour, eyes closed, meditating on my finances — rather, my lack of finances. Occasionally, the floor vibrated from the loud music on her mother's stereo.

Until I met Jess, I thought all mothers listened to Mozart, not Motown. Of course, it's hard to do aerobics to a symphony. Maybe that's why my mother never took aerobic dancing. She can't stand the music.

I opened my eyes and stretched my legs. "I already thought of getting a job. It's a dead-end idea."

"There's got to be something you could do."

"Oh yeah? Babysitting's out. My parents still hire one for me. All the lawn jobs and paper routes in the neighborhood are taken. I don't think my parents would appreciate an instant carwash in our driveway. It's too cold for a lemonade stand. And the last I heard, McDonald's doesn't hire eleven-year-olds. I rest my case."

"As usual, you're too traditional. Think of something different. You need a salable commodity."

Sometimes Jess talks more like a college senior than a sixth-grader. "Was *commodity* one of our new vocabulary words?"

I waited for her answer while she blew a bubble. "A commodity is a product people will buy."

"Like what?"

"I don't know. You'll have to figure out that part."

After two days I hadn't thought of any salable commodities. Dad suggested I make potholders. I didn't expect any great ideas from him anyway. I skipped asking my mother. I'd stayed out of her way since The Big Blowup. If Phyllis were here, she'd have five hundred suggestions. I considered writing her, but it takes too long to get a reply.

There just wasn't much a kid like me had to offer to

the world. I was beginning to think I had only one way out of this financial bind. For the next three months, I'd have to walk home from Jess's, save every cent of my "little extra," and let A.P.E. III buy my milk.

Then I remembered how long it had been since I had a butterscotch sundae with double whipped cream. And how hard it was to read a comic book cover to cover before the store manager said, "Buy it or put it down." And how disgusting Arthur was.

There was only so much I was willing to sacrifice. I *had* to make some extra money.

Gross Ed, my math teacher, has a saying he uses when a kid tells him a math problem is too difficult. "If you stop thinking about it, the solution will sneak in through the cracks in your skull."

I always thought it was just a line Gross Ed said when he wanted to read the *Wall Street Journal* instead of teaching. But I found out he was right.

It happened the next afternoon as I sat in the front seat of Violet Van. The only salable commodity on my mind was Candace Stewart's house. How I wished her parents would move out of Belmont, preferably into another time zone!

"Don't you love my new jacket, Libby?" Candace

said, as we waited for the other kids to climb in. "Mother bought it for me in New York last weekend."

"Hmmm," I replied, without turning to look. Why give her the satisfaction?

"You know, Libby, you should get your mother to help pick out your clothes." Leaning forward, she patted my red tam. "My mother says your mother has excellent taste, and it's a shame she doesn't take the time to pass some of her style on to you."

I wanted to give her a belt (in the nose), a sock (in the teeth), and a boot (out the door) to complete the outfit. But around Candace, I use tremendous self-control.

The bus monitor closed the van door, and Nora started the engine. She handed me a magazine she'd been reading. "Put this in my bag, won't you, Libby?"

As I stuck the magazine in the canvas bag at my feet, I noticed the title, *Organic Gardening*. "My grandmother used to get this."

"Is that right?" Nora said. "Did she have a vegetable garden?"

"No. Only house plants."

"Gives us good ideas for our greenhouse," she said, as we waited for the traffic light to change.

"Are you an organic florist?"

"To be honest, we sometimes cheat and use chemical sprays, but we have a beautiful compost pile out back. It makes the best soil you'd ever want to see. The potted plants love it."

Then, just the way Gross Ed said, the solution to my problem suddenly seeped through the cracks in my skull. I'd discovered my salable commodity.

"Organic gardeners use a lot of manure, don't they?" I asked.

"Is this discussion necessary?" Candace said. "It's making me ill."

"Manure is great fertilizer," Nora said. "I add it to the compost pile when I can get it. Of course, I can't put in too much or the neighbors complain."

"I bet," muttered Candace.

"Could you use about a bucketful a week, mixed with cedar shavings? It's from my guinea pigs."

"You've been holding out on me, Libby." Nora reached over and slapped my knee.

"You're both mentally deranged," Candace said.

"Can we agree on a price, Nora?"

"Oh, you're *selling* it?" She chuckled. "Well, okay. How about fifty cents a bucket?"

I was in business.

At first I took Nora a bagful three times a week after

I cleaned the cage. But Candace complained to her mother about the smell in Violet Van, and Mrs. Stewart made a fuss. Now Nora stops by my house once a week after she drops off Candace. I give it all to her then.

Despite the fact that I had an unending supply (soon to increase when Samantha's babies arrived), I could see it would take a while to pay off the $6.95 debt.

"I need a second salable commodity," I said to Jess at lunch.

"You're lucky anyone wanted your first one. I can't believe Nora is actually paying you for that stuff."

"It's cheaper and better than chemical fertilizers. I just found the right buyer."

"You are really getting into making money." She crunched a stalk of celery. "My dad says it's a disease. Once you start, you can't stop. My mother says it's too bad he never caught it."

"I'm doing it out of necessity, that's all. Once I pay back my mother, I'll have almost enough from the guinea pig manure to make up for my allowance cut."

"That's what they all say."

"Hi, Libby."

I turned to see Arthur gaping at me. "What do you want?"

"Going Halloweening tomorrow?"

"Are you for real, Arthur?" Jess rolled her eyes.

"Because if you want to," he continued, "my neighborhood is really good. They give out lots of candy. My parents will be driving me around, and they could take you too."

"He finds you irresistible, Lib." Jess snickered.

Oh, why me? Of all the boys in this world, why does it have to be A.P.E. III who finds me irresistible? Why not Ben? Why not *anybody* else?

"I don't dress up at Halloween anymore, Arthur."

"Oh." He lowered his eyes and slowly walked back to his desk. He looked pathetic.

"Sorry," I called after him.

"Totally unbelievable," Jess murmured.

"Jess!" I grabbed her by the shoulders.

"What's wrong? You have a weird look in your eyes."

"Thanks to Arthur, another idea just seeped through the cracks."

"My dad's right. It *is* a disease."

"I'll get started right away." I took a sheet of paper

from my desk. "Can I borrow your markers?"

In a few minutes my sales flier was complete. I held it up for her to see.

DID YOU GET TRICKED?
IS YOUR FRONT DOOR COVERED
WITH EGGS?
ARE YOUR CAR WINDOWS SOAPED UP?
LET LIBBY PRUITT
CLEAN UP YOUR HALLOWEEN MESS

"I'll go out tomorrow night and leave a flier at any house that gets hit."

"Clever." Jess nodded approvingly.

It was clever. It was brilliant. I hoped it would make me a bundle. I could already see the new comics piling up under my bed and taste the whipped cream and butterscotch topping.

Unfortunately, my parents insisted I stay in the neighborhood and come home by 8:30. That would definitely cut down on profits.

"Think of it as government regulation," Dad said.

As soon as the Halloweeners hit the street, I headed out armed with fliers, a bucket of soapy water, a scrub brush, and a roll of paper towels.

My first house was the Terwilligers'. When Mrs. Terwilliger answered the door, I handed her my flier. "I see your shrubs are covered with toilet paper. I'll clean it up for fifty cents."

She frowned. "You didn't, by any chance, have anything to do with this?"

"Oh no! Those kids did it." I pointed down the block to a group of boys. "I know who to follow."

"Is that so?"

"I can do it now or come back tomorrow."

She hesitated, looked me up and down, then nodded. Ten minutes later I put two quarters in my pocket and headed for the next house.

"That egg gunk on your porch will be like cement by morning," I told Mr. Angell.

He was ticked off when he saw the mess. "Okay, okay. Clean it up quick."

The evening was a great success. In an hour and a half, I made five dollars. I swept cracked corn off sidewalks, wiped shaving cream off garage doors, cleaned up smashed pumpkins, and rescued one terrified cat. And my customers were completely satisfied.

But when I saw the front of our house, I realized my brilliant plan had a minor flaw. The kids I'd been following all night had given it the royal treatment.

My mother met me at the door. She was completely *dis*satisfied.

"They must have figured out who was cleaning up after them," I groaned.

"That would be my deduction," she replied.

"I guess I have a little more work to do."

"Yes, I guess you do."

"I suppose you expect me to do it for free."

"You suppose right."

"I'll get more soap and water."

Eight

Sore Throat

• The good news is I finally have the $6.95 to pay off my mother. The bad news is I woke up this morning with a sore throat and fever.

"How could you, Libby?" my mother said, when I went into her room to announce my state of health.

She made it sound as if I'd sent out invitations to all the germs in town: PLEASE COME INFECT LIBBY PRUITT. R.S.V.P.

"I shouldn't have allowed her to tramp around all night cleaning everyone's porches," she said to my father, who was shaving in their bathroom. He grunted, then shaved his chin.

"It was scrubbing the foul words off *our* sidewalk at the end that did it." I sat down on the bed. "You shouldn't have made me do that when I was already wet."

She opened her mouth to say something, then

thought better of it. Lucky for her, too. If she dared yell at me for trying to make some extra money, I'd let her have it about my meager allowance.

"Did you take your temperature?"

"It's a hundred and two. I bet it's strep throat."

"Oh great," she muttered. "Rod, hurry up in there. We have to decide who can take Libby to the doctor's this morning."

"The number is on the bulletin board," I said.

"I know where the number is." She opened her top dresser drawer.

"I'm just trying to help. I thought since Phyllis always called the doctor, you might not know."

She handed me two throat lozenges. "Suck on these. They'll make your throat feel better."

"But Phyllis always has me gargle with salt water."

"I don't want to hear any more about Phyllis today."

I knew when to exit. I popped the lozenges in my mouth and went back to my room.

I listened to them arguing about who could best fit a sick kid into his/her schedule. My mother said she had an important case to present tomorrow and couldn't take time off today. My father insisted he had two lectures to give and a meeting with the dean and couldn't get home before 2:30. I guess my getting sick was another one of those annoying inconveniences, like the refrigerator breaking down.

In the end they decided my mother would drive me to the doctor's and stay with me until Dad could get home.

I hadn't been in for a sick visit in two years. When Phyllis hears about it, she'll say I got sick because I wasn't eating enough onions. I can't help it if Mrs. Gould thinks they stink up the house.

The office was crawling with little kids. Every one had a river of snot coming out of his nose. As soon as a mother started over to the block bin with a tissue, her kid wiped the goo with his fingers and smeared it over the blocks in front of him. I knew my mother had checked out the scene, because she led me to the chairs on the opposite side of the room.

The nurse came out and said the doctor was forty-five minutes behind schedule. My mother glanced at her watch. "Do they think we have nothing better to do than sit here?" She opened her briefcase and took out some legal papers. I think she was more worried about her stupid trial the next day than about me.

When I realized she wasn't in the mood to chat, I picked up a magazine. In the middle of an article about Princess Di, the nurse called my name.

They scheduled me with Dr. Morgan instead of Dr. Engleman, my regular pediatrician, who is a woman. This did not make me happy.

"Do I have to take off my shirt?" I asked the nurse.

"He will want to listen to your chest."

"My chest is fine. It's my throat that hurts. I don't have to take off my clothes for him to check that."

The nurse and my mother exchanged glances, then the nurse left.

"Libby, I'll be right here," my mother said. "You don't have anything to be modest about yet."

"So what? I don't want to be naked in front of him."

She gave me The Look. I sighed and removed the shirt.

My diagnosis was right. Strep throat. At least that's what Dr. Morgan said it looked like. To be sure, he did a throat culture (GAG!). He gave me medicine to take four times a day for ten days and said I couldn't go back to school for two days.

During lunch we had a thunderstorm, which is unusual for November. Maybe that's why I had a sore throat. Phyllis says it's easy to get sick during unseasonable weather.

"You go upstairs and lie down," my mother said,

after we cleaned up our dishes. "A nap will make you feel better."

A flash of lightning lit up the kitchen. "Where will you be?"

"In the study working on these papers."

A loud boom made me jump. I get nervous during thunderstorms. "I'll just lie on the couch."

"Don't be silly," she replied. "Your bed is more comfortable. It will be easier to fall asleep there."

"I really don't want to."

"Libby, it's been a hectic day, and I'm swamped with work. I'm in no mood for this."

Case closed.

It probably never occurred to her that I was afraid to go upstairs alone during the storm. She thought I'd outgrown that. Wrong.

I tried holding the pillow over my ears. Despite feeling tired and achy, I couldn't sleep. Phyllis used to sit with me and stroke my hair until I dozed off. I considered asking my mother to do that, but I knew she was too busy.

The next day my parents decided I had recovered enough to stay home alone. I know kids who would love to spend an entire day with the house to themselves. But if you ask me, it's not worth it.

All the things you like to do with no parents around you can't do anyway. Television is lousy unless you like *Sesame Street*, game shows, or soap operas (which I don't) or have cable (which we don't). You can't talk on the phone for hours because everybody else is in school. And in my case, I couldn't even pig out on junk food because there wasn't any in the house.

Still, my day had a couple of bright spots, and I'd have missed them if I'd been in school.

The first thing happened when I added fresh oatmeal to my mealworm jar. Instead of tiny, wiggly mealworms crawling around, I found three hard-shelled cylinders lying in the oatmeal. My mealworms had turned into pupas. In a couple of weeks a beetle would come out of each one. I bet mine were the first in the class to change.

After lunch I heard squealing in the basement. That's where I keep the guinea pigs when it gets cold outside. I turned on the light and saw George huddled near his water bottle. Samantha sat at the opposite corner in an odd position. Then I saw why. A baby was coming out of her.

Although she'd had other litters, I never saw the

babies being born. I sat down beside the cage. She didn't seem to mind.

It was messy to watch, but wonderful. After fifteen minutes, three babies lay beside her, two dark like George and one light brown. She cleaned them off, and soon they were on their feet, eyes open, looking for food.

As life cycles go, it beat the mealworm's by a mile.

The babies nuzzled under Samantha and began suckling. George came sniffing around. She squawked and pushed him away with her head. He retreated to his corner.

I watched all afternoon. Samantha purred as she nursed and licked them. I know it sounds weird, but the way they cuddled close to her almost made me wish I was one of her babies.

I can't understand why animals know how to be good mothers and humans don't.

DEAR PHYLLIS,

You better consider coming back to Boston. Mother and Dad are flunking parenthood.

This week I got strep throat because they made me scrub the front sidewalk in the middle of the night. Then they made me stay home all day by myself, even though I was practically delirious with a high fever.

I tried to call you yesterday, but your machine said you were in Orlando. Sam had her babies (two boys and a girl). I saw the whole thing. Real life looks a lot different than those nature films they show at school. I named them Jasmine and Cinnamon. Jess wants the third one, so she named him Bruce (after Bruce Springsteen). I like my names better.

Love, Libby
XOXOXOX

When she reads this, I thought, she'll wish she'd never gone to Florida. She'll be home by Thanksgiving. Or maybe she'll surprise me and come back in time for my birthday. That would be just like Phyllis to walk through the door as I blow out the candles.

"I wanted to make your wish come true," she'd say. "I promise never to leave again."

• Nine

Trouble Brewing

Dear Libby,

Wonderful news about the guinea pigs! Take a
picture of them with your father's Polaroid and
send it to me.

Mr. S. and I were at Disneyworld for three days
last week. It was the most fun I've had in ages.
Epcot Center was very interesting. You'd like it.

Your birthday's coming up. Do you want me to
send anything special?

Enclosed is $5. You and Jess have a sundae at the
Belmont Drugstore on me.

Love, Phyllis
XOXOXOX

Not a single word about my strep throat or what a
bad job my parents were doing! She didn't even sound
guilty about moving to Florida. I had a feeling my

dream of Phyllis coming back to me was never going to come true.

"Stop sulking. Worse things could happen," said Jess the next morning.

"Like what?" I said glumly.

"Well . . ." She chewed her gum thoughtfully. "Your parents could get divorced."

"You always say that's the best thing that ever happened to you." I hopped into Miss Harper's window seat.

"That's because together they made me miserable. Separately, they compete to see who can make me happiest."

"I don't think my parents will ever get divorced."

"Okay, it was a bad example. How about this? Miss Harper could put your desk between Candace and Natalie for the rest of the year."

"That would be awful."

"Or next to Arthur."

"Even awfuller."

"The polar ice cap could melt," she continued, "and Boston could disappear into the Atlantic."

"Enough!"

"Really. It could happen." She turned her back to

Miss Harper and blew a bubble. "Or the Soviet Union could try to eliminate all the big scientists at Harvard and M.I.T. by releasing a deadly chemical over Cambridge —"

"Stop, Jess!" I clamped my hand over her mouth.

She pulled it away. "— just as *we* go out for recess."

"Quit it. I'm not sulking anymore. See?" I stretched my lips into a huge grin.

At that, Miss Harper blinked the ceiling lights. Jess and I sat down at our desks. She handed a pile of papers to the first person in each row. "Take one and pass the rest back."

From the groans in front of me, I expected the worst. A pop quiz first thing Monday morning? I should have studied the Spanish explorers better.

I grabbed my paper. What a relief! It was only a book list. The wave of groans rippled toward the back of the room.

"Not another book report," someone grumbled.

"We just did one."

Miss Harper smiled as if she hadn't heard a single complaint. The louder the howling, the happier she is. "You'll notice the due date at the top of the sheet."

"Two weeks from today? You've got to be kidding."

"No way, José."

Her smile broadened. "Next year in the middle school, you will be expected to read a great deal. You might as well get used to it."

I scanned the list of ten books. I'd already read six of them last summer when I ran out of new comics. I decided to do *Watership Down*, since it was about rabbits.

At lunch everyone griped about how much homework we had.

"It was bad enough with math to do every night," said Tricia, "and Ms. Reinholt's science project."

"Miss Harper's crazy if she thinks we have time to read more than two hundred pages and write a report on it in two weeks," added Jess.

"If you can't take the heat, get out of the kitchen."

I didn't have to turn around to see who was talking.

"Maybe you don't belong in a school like this, Jess," Candace went on. She crossed her arms and cocked her head. "Sometimes the admissions office makes errors. This assignment should be a breeze for any capable student. Right, Natalie?"

"Well, um . . ."

I glanced at Jess to see what she would say next.

She put her hand over her mouth and sort of coughed, then dropped her hand to her side. I spotted something pink between her fingers.

"You're absolutely on target, Candace," Jess said. "Sometimes the school gets *stuck* with a real loser."

Twirling one of her curls with her finger, Candace pranced away. After a couple of steps, she stopped and looked at her shoe. A big wad of pink bubble gum stretched between her heel and the floor.

"What's wrong, Candace?" called Jess. "Are you all *stuck* up?"

Everyone turned to see what was going on. There were a few snickers when Candace tried to scrape off the gum with a pencil and got it all over her fingers. There's nothing stickier than fresh gum.

Gross Ed, who had lunch duty, looked up from his *Wall Street Journal*. "Is there a problem, Candace?" He took a gulp from his Coke can and wiped his mouth on his sleeve.

"I stepped on gum, Mr. Tisdale. I know who put it there, too."

"I'm not interested in speculation." He burped loudly.

"But it was deliberate."

"Let's not discuss your paranoia, Candace," he said

impatiently. "Here, Natalie, take the knife and help her clean it up."

"But Mr. Tisdale —" pleaded Candace.

"The rest of you remember, we have a rule about gum in school." Stuffing a large piece of meatball sandwich into his mouth, he turned the page of his newspaper.

"You're lucky, Jess," I whispered. "If it had been anybody but Gross Ed, you'd be doomed."

"She's still doomed," said Tricia. "I haven't seen Candace this mad at anyone since Marian Meezer beat her in the spelling bee in fourth grade. And you know what happened to Marian." She lowered her voice. "I think Candace is cooking up something really rotten for Jess."

"I'm not worried." Jess shrugged.

But Tricia was right. Candace was looking at Jess the way a boa constrictor looks at its next meal. You can't embarrass Candace in front of an entire class without paying for it.

That night I got the idea for another moneymaker. On a TV interview show I was watching, they spotlighted a millionaire inventor. He said the secret to success was identifying what consumers want, then giving it to them.

What the consumers in my class wanted was help finishing their book reports on time. And I could give it to them. Since I'd read over half the books, I'd sell summaries.

"I told you the smell of money was addictive." Jess shook her head.

"I'm only building a little nest egg for Christmas presents."

"Oh sure."

"I'll be doing the kids a favor."

"I don't know about this idea, Libby," she said.

"They sell book summaries in the campus bookstore. All the college students use them," I argued. "Besides, I'm not going to write the actual book reports. It'll just be a plot summary and list of characters. Like a study aid."

"It'll never work."

Jess was wrong. By Thursday I had eight clients. After school I wrote one-page summaries of six books. Then I rode my bike to the public library and made four copies of each one. Friday morning I set up business next to the forsythia bush.

Before lunch seven more kids wanted to buy summaries. The way sales were booming, I'd have to run off extra copies over the weekend.

"Maybe I should raise prices." I said to Jess, while we changed for gym class. "That's what stores do when demand increases."

She rolled her eyes. "Libby, you're getting carried away with this."

"I'll make a mint next week off the kids who haven't read their books yet. They'll pay just about anything I ask."

"Hurry up and get your sneakers on or you'll be late."

"I think I'll read a couple of the other books over the weekend. That would boost sales. Give the consumer more selection," I said, as we lined up for attendance.

Mr. Lynch divided us into teams for volleyball. As I headed across the gym to my net, Ben tapped me on the shoulder. I was surprised. Although he's not as shy with me since our mealworm jar adventure, he never talks to me in gym class.

"Libby, about your book summaries —"

So that was it! Even Ben couldn't resist such a great offer. "I only have *Huckleberry Finn* and *Jane Eyre* left, but I'll have more on Monday. Today they're a dollar. The price might go up next week." A shrewd businesswoman can't afford to play favorites.

He shook his head. "No, I don't want to buy one."

"What then?"

"I thought you should know." He leaned close to my ear (heavenly!) and whispered, "On the way to gym, I saw Candace go into Mr. Ashley's office with one of your summaries."

• Ten

A Silver Lining

• Mr. Ashley's office is on the main hall. Outside, next to his door, is a red wooden bench. If a kid is sitting on the bench, you know he's in major trouble.

At three o'clock Friday afternoon the kid on that bench was me.

The dismissal bell rang and the entire school population paraded by. I tried to hide behind a library book. It didn't work.

"Hey, Libby, what'd you do?"

"Look, Libby Pruitt's on the hot seat."

"I tried to warn you, Lib." Jess stood in front of me.

"It was that creep Candace." I clenched my fist.

"You'd have gotten caught anyhow."

I stared at her in disbelief. "You're sticking up for her?"

"Are you kidding?" She scrunched up her face as if she'd sucked a lemon. "But don't you see? Miss

Harper would have known when all the reports came in sounding alike."

I sighed. "I never thought of that."

Jess pointed to the door. "Who's in there?"

"My mother. And is she steamed! She had to leave work early because Mr. Ashley wanted the meeting today."

"Not a good situation." Jess clicked her tongue.

"She kept saying, 'I never expected something like this from you.'"

Jess shrugged. "It's *exactly* what I'd expect from you."

"Thanks a lot." I peered through the curtained window into Mr. Ashley's office. "What do you think they're talking about?"

"Probably trying to figure out a just and meaningful punishment."

The door knob turned.

"Call me tonight," Jess said. Giving me the thumbs-up sign, she ran down the hall.

My mother came out of the office. She was not smiling. She didn't speak until we reached the car. "How could you do such a thing?" She gripped the steering wheel.

"I was trying to be an entrepreneur." That was on

the week's vocabulary list. "I didn't think anyone would mind."

"You didn't think, period."

I removed the red tam and laid it in my lap. If only Phyllis were here. She'd understand.

I flipped on the radio. Frowning, my mother turned it off. We drove on in silence.

"What are you going to do to me?" I asked, as we turned onto Elm Street.

"You'll give back the money, of course. And apologize to your class."

Not that! I thought in horror. Selling the summaries was a stupid thing to do. I should have realized that it was the same as cheating. But I didn't *mean* to do anything wrong. Please, don't make me apologize in front of my class. "I'll feel like a fool," I said to her.

She glanced at me and raised one eyebrow. "Mr. Ashley and I agreed that you must have too much free time on your hands if you could manage to do all this extra work."

Uh oh.

"He suggested we enroll you in the After-School Program. I think it's an excellent idea."

"I'd hate it. They have dumb stuff like Square Dancing and Healthful Cooking. I won't go!"

"Oh yes you will," she said sharply. She parked the car in our driveway and shut off the engine. "Why do you have to be so difficult about everything? You can at least look at the list of activities."

"I never had to do things like this before Phyllis left, and I'm not doing it now!" Glaring at her, I unhooked my seatbelt.

"Libby, please don't keep acting this way with me." Her voice cracked.

As I slammed the car door, I saw her lay her forehead against the steering wheel. I think she might have been crying.

She didn't come into the house for a long time.

I knew I was a disappointment to my mother. A person like her shouldn't have a daughter like me. I get sick at the wrong times. I'm still afraid of thunderstorms. I do silly things like getting my hand stuck in mealworm jars.

She wants me to read good books instead of comics. When I do, I'm almost kicked out of school.

She wants me to be independent and self-reliant. But taking care of myself makes me feel lonely and scared.

She wants me to be perfect like she is, and I keep making mistakes.

*   *   *

Monday morning, after the Pledge of Allegiance, I had to stand in front of the class and apologize for my book summary scheme. I shut my eyes and pretended to be in my bedroom talking to the walls. It didn't help. I was still humiliated.

At first most kids felt sorry for me. Then Miss Harper handed out a revised book list and said she wouldn't accept any reports on the six books I'd summarized. That was the end of the sympathy.

They might have given me the silent treatment for a week, if Jess hadn't spread the word that Candace squealed. Without mentioning that we'd all have been in trouble when Miss Harper read the reports, Jess convinced everyone that Candace, not me, was the one to blame. Since nobody wanted to tangle with Candace, the Book Summary Fiasco was over.

Almost. I was still trapped in the After-School Program. I finally decided on Recorder Assemble, because it was the only thing on the list that didn't sound totally bo-oring. I figured learning how to build audio-visual equipment might be interesting.

Then on the drive home in Violet Van, Meghan told me it was Recorder *Ens*emble and the recorders were musical instruments, not A.V. stuff. *And* the woman who taught it made you practice at home. Horrible!

It was too late to get out of the class. My mother had already signed my life away.

After a start like that, the week would have earned a zero (on a scale of one to ten) except for a few bright spots. Instead it gets a four minus.

Point #1 is for the fun I had watching Jasmine, Cinnamon, and Bruce run around the basement with Samantha and George. They all formed a line nose to rear and scampered across the floor. One day Bruce hid under the oil tank. It took two hours to coax him out. That's where the minus comes from.

Point #2 is for the mealworms. The pupas finally turned into beetles. I don't like them as much as the mealworms, because they move too fast to hold and they're ugly. The good part is they'll lay eggs, and I'll end up with even more mealworms.

Some of the kids don't want to keeps theirs now that we've seen the entire life cycle. So I've adopted four other jars. I might start a mealworm supply company. I read that pet stores sell mealworms as fish and lizard food. Since a single female lays five hundred eggs, I could make a fortune.

The rest of the week's points go to — hard to believe — Recorder Ensemble. It wasn't as terrible as I expected. Molly, the teacher, is a college student who works in the After-School Program to earn extra money. She wants us to enjoy ourselves and doesn't mind if we make mistakes, as long as we try hard.

Not that I'm *glad* my mother made me do this two days a week. It's better than sitting around an empty house waiting for my parents to get home, but it's not as good as hanging around with Jess.

Ten kids are in the group. The good news is one of them is Ben. The bad news is another is Candace.

"Libby has to take this because she got caught cheating," she told Molly my first day.

Molly looked shocked. She probably thought I was a "problem child."

"You don't know what you're talking about, Candace," I said.

"Oh really?" She put her hands on her hips. "You want us to believe it's a coincidence you suddenly signed up?"

"Well . . ." I tried to think of a good response.

At that moment Ben came up beside me. "Libby planned to join ever since I told her how much fun it was. Right, Lib?"

I smiled at him gratefully.

"I'm glad Ben has been recruiting for our group."
Molly patted my shoulder. "Libby, which recorder
do you want to learn — alto or soprano?"

I pointed to Candace's. "What kind is hers?"

"Alto."

"I'll take soprano."

Molly handed me the plastic recorder, which re-
sembled a white clarinet. She gestured to the chair
at one end of the semicircle. "Why don't you sit next
to Ben? He's our best soprano. He can help you with
the fingerings."

Two points!

Eleven

Birthday Surprise

• "Want to hear 'Twinkle, Twinkle, Little Star'?" I asked Jess as she came down the basement stairs.

"Why are you practicing here?"

"It sounds better. Listen." I blew into my recorder. "Great echo, eh?"

"I guess so." She reached into the guinea pig cage and scooped up Bruce.

Turning the page in the music book to "Twinkle, Twinkle," I put the recorder to my lips. On the first note the guinea pigs began squealing.

"The pigs don't carry a tune too well, but you're not bad," said Jess. "I didn't know you had any musical ability."

"I practiced hard over Thanksgiving break. Molly says if I keep improving, I'll be good enough to play in the holiday concert."

"I'll be right back." She ran upstairs and returned with a box wrapped in red-and-yellow-striped paper. "Happy twelfth birthday! I know it's not until tomorrow, but I'll be with my dad then."

"Thanks, Jess." I tore off the paper. Inside was a wood cutout of my name stained dark brown and varnished.

"It's for your bedroom door."

"You made it?"

She smiled proudly. "I did it in my dad's workshop."

"It's great." I swabbed my recorder dry and placed it in the carrying case. "Come on. I'll show you what Phyllis sent me."

"Your mom's not home. Can I bring Bruce upstairs?"

"Okay. But if he messes, you clean it up."

I opened the box on the kitchen table and lifted out the ice cream maker. "It came today. I can't wait to try it."

"Six different topping flavors!" Jess picked up one of the jars. "Yummy! You're lucky to have a grandmother like Phyllis. Mine sends hideous sweaters every year."

"Look, she even sent Marshmallow Fluff." I unscrewed the top, and we stuck our fingers in for a sample.

"What are your parents getting you?"

"Dad's giving me a new wallet. I picked it out last weekend."

"How appropriate!" She laughed. "I hope it's big enough."

"My mother's taking me out tomorrow for some clothes and a surprise, whatever that means. Then the three of us are going to The Oyster House and a movie."

"Sounds decent to me."

"Yeah, I suppose." I shrugged. "I just wish Phyllis were here."

Jess licked a second helping of Fluff off her finger. "So tell me, how does it feel to be on the threshold of adolescence?"

"Don't rush me. I'm not there yet."

"You mean you're not dying to have zits and hairy armpits?"

"Why do you have to put it *that* way?"

"Because that's the way it is."

I'm not sure I'm ready for all the things that will start happening to me soon. It's not only getting my period or growing hair in new places that bothers me. It's what everyone expects when those things happen.

Teenage girls are supposed to read *Seventeen*, not Marvel comics. They watch MTV, not Saturday morning cartoons. They spend hours putting on makeup, not playing with guinea pigs. They drink diet soda and eat cottage cheese, not milkshakes and ice cream sundaes.

What if I don't *want* to do the things I'm supposed to want to do?

It's happening already. My parents tell me I'm old enough to take care of myself when they're not around. Mr. Ashley tells me I can only have one recess, because sixth graders are too grown up for two. And my teachers tell me it's time to work harder, because next year I'll be in middle school.

Why does everyone keep pushing me to change when I like things the way they are?

The next morning my mother and I hit every clothing store in the mall. We gave pounding headaches to at least ten salesgirls. It wasn't my fault. I knew exactly what I wanted. The problem was that my mother knew exactly what she wanted me to want. Since it was my birthday present we were buying, I think I should have won. It didn't work that way. We ended up with three bags of clothes neither one of us liked.

After lunch at Burger King (I had a Whopper, she had the salad bar), we drove toward home.

"We have one more stop to make," she said cheerfully. "My surprise for you." She was really excited.

I was too. Should I think big like new furniture for my bedroom? No, Dad would've come along for that. Maybe something smaller, like my own television.

She drove into downtown Belmont and pulled into a parking space. I examined the stores for a clue. Florist, drugstore, gift shop.

"You have a one-thirty appointment," she said, digging through her purse for parking meter change.

"Appointment for what?"

"To have your hair done. Any style you want."

"Done?"

"Jackie — you know, my hairdresser — is terrific. She does very cute cuts for girls your age."

My mouth dropped open. "This is your fantastic surprise?"

Smiling, she nodded.

"It's a gag gift, right? It worked. I'm gagging."

"I thought you'd be pleased."

"I like my hair the way it is. I don't want a cute cut

or a stunning style or anything else." I sat back in my seat and crossed my arms. No way was I going in there.

"I tried to think of something you'd enjoy." She rubbed the palms of her hands on the steering wheel. "On my twelfth birthday, Phyllis did this for me. I thought it was wonderful. I felt grown up having my hair done."

"In case you didn't notice, I'm not like you," I said coolly. "And for your information, Phyllis would never, ever do this to *me*."

"I'm sorry, Libby." Her voice was nearly a whisper. "I thought you'd like my surprise." She touched my arm. I pulled it away.

Then she sighed — a loud, exaggerated sigh designed to make me feel guilty. Well, it didn't work. I turned my head and stared out the side window.

I knew I'd hurt her feelings, but I didn't care. It was *my* birthday, and she'd ruined it.

After a minute or two, she gave up and went into the hairdresser's to cancel the appointment. When she came out, she didn't say a word. No sighs, no lectures, no yelling. Nothing. Total silence the whole way home.

Twelve

The Frame-Up

• One of the things I like about school is how it helps you forget your problems at home.

When I sit in math staring at Ben's hands and half-listening to Gross Ed yell at us for messing up the word problem assignment, it's easy to erase unpleasant thoughts. Like the one about my mother being sorry she had a kid like me.

While I'm watching a filmstrip about Ponce de Leon, I pretend that Phyllis is home baking my favorite cookies for an afternoon snack.

When I'm looking at pond water through the microscope, I imagine that my father has given up all his mathematical formulas, never lets details slip his mind, and always hears me when I talk to him.

Then there are times when the problems at school get so big, I don't have a chance to worry about home. Like this Monday.

When we came in from recess, Mr. Ashley was standing next to Miss Harper at the front of the classroom. The minute everyone spotted him, the laughing and chattering stopped. We slipped quietly, and nervously, into our seats.

"I wonder what's going on? Ashley looks upset," Tricia whispered.

I thought about Jess, who was in Maine with her father until Wednesday. She'd be sorry she missed this. She thinks a crisis is exciting.

"Miss Harper informs me that there has been a series of thefts in this class," Mr. Ashley began. His eyes moved up and down each row, staring at every kid, one by one. Even though I didn't know anything about the thefts, he made me feel guilty.

"At first the amounts involved were small — only lunch money."

Behind me, someone sneezed three times in a row. It sounded funny, but nobody laughed.

"On Friday," he continued, "Arthur had ten dollars taken from his backpack. When he was ready to go home, he discovered the loss."

Miss Harper stepped forward. "Mr. Ashley and I suspect someone in this room is responsible for these thefts." She paused and scanned our faces just as Mr.

Ashley had. "If the guilty party comes forward now, the punishment will be less severe."

You could have heard a cottonball hit the floor.

"You may admit your guilt privately, of course. I'll be in my office," Mr. Ashley said. "Be sure of this — we have ways of catching the thief. And we will use them."

No one moved a muscle until he and Miss Harper stepped into the hall.

Tricia leaned across the aisle. "Who do you think did it?"

"I don't know, but whoever it is probably won't be a student here after they catch him," I said.

Last period, most of the class went to the library to research science reports. I stayed behind to copy over my book report in ink. In the middle of the first page, my pen went dry.

None of the five kids in the room had a pen. Miss Harper was in the office, and I knew she wouldn't like me borrowing one of hers without asking. Then I remembered Jess kept one in her desk. I opened the top, expecting to see a pen. Instead, I saw something else.

I slammed her desk top shut. My hands were shaking. My heart could have qualified for the Guinness

Book as fastest and loudest nonartificial beater.

I looked around the room. Nobody was watching. I lifted the top again to be sure I wasn't dreaming. Sitting neatly on Jess's math book was a plastic sandwich bag. Inside was a ten-dollar bill, a couple of dollars, and some change.

Jess never brought money to school. It had to be the stolen loot. Of course, Jess wasn't the thief. No question about that. Even if she were, she was too smart to go away for three days and leave the money where Miss Harper would surely find it in a desk search.

It began to make sense. The real thief wanted Jess caught. Everyone knew she would be absent this week. But only one person would want her accused of stealing and kicked out of school.

Candace.

I knew it was only a matter of time before she went after Jess. Jess had made a fool of Candace too many times and had stood up to her *way* too many times. It all boiled down to one thing: Jess wasn't afraid of Candace, and Candace hated her for it.

Someone had to stop Candace Stewart. But what to do?

It wouldn't help to show the money to Miss Harper. She'd never believe her darling Candace would steal. I couldn't leave the money where it was. I could put it in Candace's desk and hope *she* got caught. But I knew as soon as she saw it, she'd plant it back in Jess's desk.

Maybe if I'd had more time to think, I could have hit upon a better solution. But time was running out. Soon Miss Harper would be back and the rest of the class would return from the library. I had to act fast.

Reaching in, I picked up the bag. I stuffed it in my desk under the science book and watched the clock slowly tick off the minutes. At last the dismissal bell rang.

If I was lucky, I could drop the bag of money onto Miss Harper's desk and slip out before anyone saw. And if I stayed lucky, Candace wouldn't figure out who ruined her plan. If she did, I was history.

I waited until everyone left. Then I made my move. Keeping my eye on Miss Harper, who stood in the hall outside the room talking to the librarian, I pulled out the bag and hurried toward her desk.

Just as I tossed it on her blotter, a voice behind me screamed. "Miss Harper! Miss Harper!"

I spun around. Candace and Natalie pointed at me.

"What's wrong?" Miss Harper ran into the room. "Is someone hurt?"

"Natalie and I were coming out of the cloakroom and saw Libby put that on your desk," Candace said.

When Miss Harper bent down to examine the plastic bag, Candace's innocent smile turned to a smirk. I felt like wrapping her earmuffs around her neck.

Miss Harper held up the money. Candace's sweet expression returned. "Libby, did you put this here?"

"Yes, Miss Harper. But it's not how it looks."

"Well?"

I cleared my throat. "I, uh, found it."

"Where?" Her voice told me I was getting in deeper every second.

I didn't want to pull Jess's name into the discussion. That's exactly what Candace wanted. "In the classroom. The thief placed it so someone else would get in trouble."

"Really?" she said skeptically.

I glanced at Candace. She gave me her snake look. This time *I* was the mouse.

I wasn't going to let her scare me. "Miss Harper, I'll tell you who the thief is. It's —"

The snake bared her fangs and hissed. "I didn't

want to say anything before," interrupted Candace, "because I hoped Libby would confess. But Natalie and I saw her steal Arthur's ten dollars on Friday. Didn't we, Natalie?"

Natalie nodded.

"Come, Libby," Miss Harper said. "You're going to see Mr. Ashley. And, Candace and Natalie, thank you very much."

I should have known better than to tangle with a snake.

I sat on the red wooden bench for a half hour until Mr. Ashley contacted one of my parents. As usual, Dad didn't answer his phone. Mother was in court. When he finally reached her, she said she couldn't get to the school for forty-five minutes.

While we waited, Mr. Ashley and I had our little talk. He wouldn't listen to me. After the book summary incident, my reputation with him was tarnished. As soon as he found out Candace and Natalie had "witnessed" the theft, my case was lost.

Eventually, my mother arrived. Her meeting with Mr. Ashley was short, but the ten-minute drive home seemed like ten hours.

"If you needed money, you should have asked me," she said, when we got in the house.

"But I didn't do it." I took off my red tam and jacket.

"Imagine what Mr. Ashley must think of your father and me."

"Aren't you listening? I didn't steal the money."

"This is serious, Libby. There were witnesses. Unless you admit your guilt, Mr. Ashley will expel you from school."

"I'm not going to admit to something I didn't do," I cried. "Candace lied. She never saw me take Arthur's money. I found it in Jess's desk, and I know *she* didn't steal it. I was returning it to Miss Harper when Candace squealed."

"Candace Stewart? That's Madeline Stewart's daughter, isn't it? Now, Libby, why on earth would she lie?"

How could my mother think *I'd* do something like that? "I wish Phyllis were here. She knows I'd never steal. If you paid more attention to me . . . if you weren't always working . . . you'd know too!"

"That's not fair. I give you all the time I possibly can."

"Meghan's father is a lawyer, and he doesn't work as much as you do."

"I got a late start. I have a lot of catching up to do."

We all knew whose fault *that* was. I tried to swallow the lump in my throat, but it kept creeping back. "If Phyllis were here, she'd —"

My mother grabbed my shoulders. "I'm sick of hearing what Phyllis would do. Phyllis is not your mother. I am."

"Then why don't you believe me?" I was angry and hurt and scared. Twisting loose, I made a dash for my bedroom.

• Thirteen

Caught Purple-Handed

• Next morning when I came down for breakfast, I found my parents sitting at the kitchen table sipping coffee as though it was Sunday. Something was up.

"We'll be driving you to school," my mother said.

"I thought you had a meeting this morning," I said hesitantly.

"I've delayed the meeting."

Uh oh. That meant it was something *really* serious. Maybe Mr. Ashley called in the police.

She dumped the last of her coffee into the sink. "I made a mistake, and I plan to correct it. Dad and I discussed this last night, and he agrees it's the right thing to do."

My father reached across the table and patted my hand. "We're going to demand that Ashley conduct a formal hearing, so you can tell your side of the story."

I couldn't believe my ears.

My mother continued, "We'll expect him to allow other people to testify on your behalf."

"Like Jess?"

"Yes. And I want to ask Candace and Natalie a few questions about their accusation, since apparently no one else has bothered."

"But yesterday you wanted me to plead guilty. You thought —"

"I'm sorry about yesterday. I know you'd never steal." She sounded embarrassed. I couldn't remember her ever sounding embarrassed. "I handled the whole thing badly. I should have insisted on hearing your side while I was in Ashley's office. Don't worry, we'll straighten this out."

I didn't understand what came over my mother. But whatever it was, it happened just in time. Mr. Ashley was ready to fry me.

Everyone noticed when my parents showed up at Mr. Ashley's office.

"Candace is spreading it around that you stole that money," Tricia said, as I hung up my coat. "She says your parents are here to pick up your records, because you're getting kicked out."

"She would," I muttered.

"I don't think you stole anything."

"Thanks, Tricia. I wish Mr. Ashley didn't either."

The news traveled fast. I kept hearing whispers behind my back. When I spoke to certain kids, they walked away. Even Arthur snubbed me.

I felt like hiding so I wouldn't have to face them. But since I knew that would make me look guilty, I tried to ignore it.

When it was time to go to math, Ben stopped by my desk. "I know you're innocent." He looked me right in the eye, and I was sure he meant it. "I hope they catch the real thief soon."

I felt better after that.

As I started to enter Gross Ed's room, my dad called my name. The meeting with Mr. Ashley was over.

"Good news," he said, as I ran down the hall toward them. "Ashley's agreed to the hearing."

My mother beamed. "It will be this Friday. Jess should be back by then, right?"

I nodded. Things were looking up. Not only would I get to clear myself, but we'd have a chance to nail Candace, too. Best of all, my parents — even though they are very busy people — were taking the time to fight for me.

"Everything will work out fine, Libby," said Mother. Then, right in the middle of the crowded hall, she kissed my forehead.

Phyllis would *never* have done that. She knew how embarrassing it is to have your mother kiss you in public. Mother had a lot to learn. Well, you can't expect miracles.

I smiled and let her do it.

When Jess returned to school on Thursday, I told her the whole story.

"It's rotten that Candace went after you," she fumed. "I'm the one she wants to get even with. I hope your mother is a good lawyer. You know what Mr. Ashley and Miss Harper think of darling Candace."

I hoped my mother could pull it off, too. It wouldn't be easy. My parents found out that Mrs. Stewart complained to the Board of Trustees when she heard that Candace would be questioned. Then Mr. Ashley told Mother that he might not let her ask Candace anything.

At eleven o'clock that morning something happened to make me forget my hearing. It was silent reading time. I was in the middle of a chapter when the lights blinked.

"Class," said Miss Harper, "I have just discovered that all the money I collected for your paperback book orders is gone. It was in a wallet in my desk drawer earlier this morning. It's not there now."

Voices buzzed. I didn't have to look to know everybody was staring at me. I wanted to shout, "Candace did it!" but I stopped myself. It wouldn't help my case to accuse her. Some people might believe me, but others — like Miss Harper — would think I was guiltier than ever.

"If the money is not returned before the end of the day, I'm afraid I will have to take serious action. We will not tolerate theft in this school."

"I have a bad feeling about this," Jess said, when we were dismissed for lunch. "I knew Candace would try something before the hearing. This might be it."

I followed her into the cloakroom to get our bag lunches. "I'm in big trouble, I know that. Did you see the way Miss Harper was staring at me?"

As I reached into my cubby for my bag, Miss Harper burst into the cloakroom. "Jess, I think you'd better open your backpack."

"Why?" Jess squared her shoulders.

"Someone reported seeing you place a suspicious object in it," she replied.

I noticed Natalie behind her.

"Will you open it, or do I have to call Mr. Ashley?"

"Okay, okay." Jess unzipped her pouch.

"There it is," shouted Natalie. "Like I told you."

Miss Harper held up a plastic bag full of money. "Let's go, Jess." She pointed to the door. "You're going to the office."

The snake strikes again.

I couldn't eat. It made me sick to watch Candace and Natalie bragging to anyone who would listen about how they captured the thieves. They were really enjoying themselves. Especially Candace.

Poor Jess. And poor me. No telling what would happen to us now. After this, Mr. Ashley would never believe we were innocent. Too bad Candace wasn't *shaped* like a snake. I'd love to tie her into a barrel knot.

The next thing I knew, Jess came through the door. She pulled me aside. "I'm exonerated!" she whispered.

"Oh no! Maybe your parents will get him to change his mind."

She grinned. "You haven't studied your vocabulary

list again. It means I'm cleared. Ashley knows I didn't do it."

"How? I don't get it. Why didn't he believe *me*?"

Before she could answer, the ceiling lights flickered. Mr. Ashley stood in the doorway. In his hands he held a peculiar kind of lamp. He placed it on Miss Harper's desk and plugged it in.

"What's that for?" someone asked.

He didn't explain. "I'd like you all to line up."

I turned to Jess. "Aren't you coming?"

"Don't have to."

I was about to ask why, when Miss Harper told me to get in line. Mr. Ashley instructed each person to place his hands under the light. He looked at the hands, then called the next kid in line. What was this all about?

Candace approached the desk. "Will this light give me a suntan, Mr. Ashley?" she joked.

"Please put your hands here," he replied soberly.

A second later, Candace screamed. "Help me! My hands! What's wrong with them?"

We all crowded around to see. Under the light her hands had turned purple.

"Looks as though we've found who stole your book money," Mr. Ashley said to Miss Harper.

"What are you talking about?" cried Candace. "Jess is the thief."

"The money in Miss Harper's desk was dusted with an invisible chemical. It sticks to the hands and won't wash off. Under this special light it shows up purple." He shook his head. "I'd say you touched that money, Candace. Jess's hands were clean."

"But, Mr. Ashley, there must be a mistake."

Ignoring her protests, he pulled her toward his office. He motioned for Miss Harper to bring Natalie.

Natalie thrust her hands under the light. "See. I didn't steal anything," she whimpered. "Candace did it all. Arthur's ten dollars, the lunch money, the book order. She made me blame Libby and Jess."

Taking her arm, Miss Harper led her out.

"Give me five, Lib!" Jess cheered.

I slapped her palm with mine. "At last someone outfoxed the snake!"

Fourteen

Off with the Hat

• That was the end of Candace. The rumor is her parents sent her away to a fancy boarding school in New Hampshire. It's not as far as I'd hoped for, but it'll do.

As for Natalie, Mr. Ashley made her wash blackboards every day until winter break. With Candace gone, she isn't so obnoxious. She even apologized to Jess and me.

The other news is that Jasmine, Cinnamon, and Bruce have moved away from home. Meghan took Jasmine, and a fourth-grader has Cinnamon. Bruce lives in a deluxe cage (thanks to Jess's father) and stays in Jess's room (thanks to her mother).

I think Samantha misses them a little, but not for long. She's pregnant again. Anybody who thinks rabbits are the fastest reproducers hasn't met my guinea pigs.

Speaking of mothers, mine surprised me the other day. This is what happened.

It was two Saturdays after the stolen money episode. I was in my room counting how many new mealworms had hatched in the past couple of weeks. My mother knocked on my open door. She carried a large blue plastic box.

"What's that?" I asked, as I dumped the oatmeal and mealworms back into the mayonnaise jar.

"I saw this in Bradlee's. It's for storing sweaters. I thought — I hoped — maybe you could use it for your comic books." She looked at me expectantly.

Taking it from her hands, I examined the box. It had a lid and was roomy enough to hold all my comics plus a bunch of new ones. It could slide under my bed and wouldn't fall apart like the cardboard one. Mrs. Gould couldn't possibly mistake it for trash.

"Thanks," I said. "This will work fine."

"Good." She sounded relieved. "Um, mind if I sit down?"

"Go ahead."

Sitting on my bed, she cleared her throat and nervously fingered her wedding ring. "I know it's been difficult for you since Phyllis left."

Staring into my mealworm jar, I nodded.

"It's been a little — more than a little — hard for me, as well," she continued. "It takes time to adjust to changes like that, and" — she paused, then took a deep breath — "I miss her."

How about that? It never occurred to me that my mother might miss Phyllis, too.

"I know I don't do things as well as Phyllis did," she said, "but I'm trying."

I was sorry I'd made a fuss over the haircut. I guess that was the best birthday surprise she could think of. I pointed to the plastic box. "You're improving."

She smiled.

For a few minutes, neither of us said anything. I stared into the mealworm jar again.

"I'll let you get back to whatever you were doing." She stood up. "Dad suggested a family trip to the Aquarium this afternoon if you'd like."

"I love the Aquarium! I haven't been there since Phyllis —" I stopped myself. "Yes. Let's go."

She walked toward the door. "I'll tell him."

She was almost out in the hall when I remembered. "Wait. I want to ask you something."

She leaned against the door frame.

"What about the holiday concert at school? Molly says I'm good enough to be in the recorder ensemble."

"I saw the notice you brought home," she said. "Dad will go. He doesn't have classes Friday."

"I want you to be there, too."

"I'm sorry, Libby. I have a court hearing scheduled for Friday afternoon. If it weren't court, I'd reschedule. But other people are involved, and I have to be there."

I bit my lip so it wouldn't quiver. I don't know why I was upset. My mother never went to school activities during the day. She had obligations. That hadn't changed. It would never change.

Still, since she was trying to do better, I thought maybe this time . . .

She put her arm around my shoulders. "How about playing your part for me now?"

I shook my head. "It would sound stupid. I don't play the melody."

"Oh." She thought a minute. "We could have Dad record the concert. I can listen to it when I get home."

"I haven't forgotten how he missed recording my birth. Do you think we can trust him to hit the right button?"

"Well . . ." she said slowly.

We looked at each other, then burst out laughing. It felt good to share a joke with her.

After she went downstairs, I put my comics in the new box. Phyllis would think it was terrific. I decided to mail her a photo of it. If my dad didn't goof up, I'd send her a tape of the concert, too.

I picked up the red tam from my dresser. Placing it on my head, I looked at myself in the mirror. "No, it doesn't do a thing for you," I said aloud. "It doesn't even keep your head warm."

I removed the hat and stuffed it in the back of my bottom drawer. I knew Phyllis would understand.

The holiday concert was a big success. All the kids who play instruments performed, and the cafeteria was packed with parents. I watched the door, thinking my mother might walk in. She didn't.

The recorder ensemble got lots of applause. Molly was proud of us. She came backstage after our performance and shook everybody's hand. Then she said how she hoped we all would continue with the ensemble during spring semester.

"Are you going to stay in the group after the holidays?" Ben asked me, while we swabbed our recorders.

"Probably. I like it," I replied. "Are you?"

Smiling, he nodded. "You played great, Libby."

I made five mistakes, and I knew he heard them. But, for me, that *was* great. "Thanks for helping me learn, Ben," I said.

"Maybe now that you know how" — pausing, he raised his eyebrows — "we could practice together sometimes."

"You mean, like duets?" I asked.

"Yes. We could play duets."

·I grinned at him, and he grinned at me. It was great. If Dad hadn't come to get me, we might have stood grinning at each other for hours.

Who needs fifty VW Beetles, anyway?

On the way home, I checked the tape and found that Dad had managed to push the right button and record the entire concert. When Mother came home from her court hearing, we listened to it. Then my parents took me to the Belmont Drugstore to celebrate with a chocolate chip sundae with butterscotch topping and double whipped cream.

Don't get the idea that all my days are that good. I still come home to an empty house most afternoons. My mother still won't buy me Marshmallow Fluff. My father still gets so involved in his formulas that he forgets I'm around.

And I still miss Phyllis. But only sometimes.